BENEATH THE SUNSET & STARS

PRITOM BARMAN

Made with ♥ on the Notion Press Platform
www.notionpress.com

"To all the overthinkers out there—you are not alone!"

Contents

Contents

Preface

Hello, dear readers!

I'm Pritom Barman, and I'm excited to share *Beneath the Sunset & Stars* with you. Writing this novel has been a heartfelt journey filled with discovery, love, and more than a few awkward moments that I believe many of you can relate to.

Growing up between the breathtaking landscapes of Arunachal Pradesh and the vibrant culture of Assam, I have always been captivated by stories—whether they were found in the rich folklore of my surroundings, the books I devoured, or the tales shared by friends and family. My passion for storytelling blossomed as I navigated the ups and downs of life, leading me to the world of writing where I could pour my thoughts, emotions, and experiences onto the page.

This novel draws inspiration from my own experiences with love, relationships, and the delightful chaos that life often brings. The characters of Gaurav and Prakriti mirror my journey—filled with heartfelt moments, friendship, and the occasional humorous mishap. And yes, Hardy the turtle is inspired by my own quirky pet, who always seems to have a knack for getting into trouble!

Beneath the Sunset & Stars is a celebration of the moments that make life beautiful and messy. It's about embracing imperfections, finding laughter in unexpected places, and cherishing the connections we form along the way. I hope this story brings a smile to your face and warmth to your heart, just as writing it has done for me.

Thank you for joining me on this adventure. I can't wait for you to dive into Gaurav and Prakriti's story, and I hope

you enjoy every moment of it!
    With love,
Pritom

Acknowledgements

I would like to extend my heartfelt thanks to everyone who has supported me throughout the journey of writing this novel. To my family and friends, your unwavering encouragement and understanding have been my greatest motivation. You stood by me during the late nights and countless revisions, and I am forever grateful for your belief in me.

A special thank you goes to my writing group. Your invaluable feedback, insightful critiques, and late-night brainstorming sessions kept me inspired and focused. I truly couldn't have done this without your support.

To my muse, Prakriti, thank you for being the light that guided me through the creative process. Your love and inspiration breathed life into these characters and helped me tell this story. This book is for you.

This novel marks my second attempt at publishing after a long hiatus. The last book I wrote was back in 2011 during my school days, a time when I had no idea how to navigate the world of publishing. That first book, My Broken Heart, was published through KDP (Kindle Direct Publishing), thanks to a nudge from my dear school friend, Simi. She believed in my writing even when I was uncertain, and her suggestion to try self-publishing opened a door I hadn't considered. Without her encouragement, I might not have taken that first step.

The road to this book was not without its challenges. I faced many ups and downs along the way, including the loss of my primary laptop, which meant I lost a significant portion of my manuscript. But through determination and resilience, I worked hard to recreate and refine my vision. It took time, but I am proud of what I have accomplished.

I am especially grateful to my parents for their constant support and encouragement. To my brother, Upam Barman, you have been my rock and my first cheerleader. The moment I told you I was writing again, your excitement fueled my passion. You said, "Are you writing it again?" and that simple question ignited a fire within me.

I also want to thank Dharitry for the inspiration and for believing in me when I needed it most. And finally, a heartfelt thank you to all the readers who made this manuscript possible. Your enthusiasm and support mean the world to me.

This journey has been one of growth, passion, and discovery, and I am excited to share this story with all of you. Thank you for being a part of it.

Prologue

Coffee, Cigarettes, and Cosmic Coincidences

It all started a few years back, but honestly, it still feels as fresh as yesterday. Now, I could start this story with a typical "Once upon a time" spiel, but let's be real: life isn't a fairy tale. My story? Oh, it's messy, it's weird, and trust me, it's going to be worth the ride if you stick around.

But before we jump to the part where my world flips upside down—yeah, the big love story and all that jazz—let's rewind a bit, because you need context. I mean, who doesn't love a good setup? Don't get me wrong, my life wasn't some tragic rom-com setup where I wandered around looking for love in all the wrong places. I was doing fine. But you know how it is—when you meet *that* person, the one who makes everything click, suddenly, all the "just fine" moments in life feel like they were missing something. Spoiler alert: that missing something was her.

And then there's this thing about the universe. Yeah, you know how it loves to meddle. Sometimes, it's like the universe is sitting in a director's chair, yelling "ACTION!" while writing your story with golden ink.

Let me set the scene: Tezpur, of all places. Picture a wooden balcony overlooking the Brahmaputra River, the sun casting golden rays as it sinks into the horizon. And there I am—yours truly—sitting dramatically, cigarette in my left hand, coffee mug in my right, rocking my best black outfit, because why not? Oh, and there's a ukulele casually chilling on the chair next to me, giving off "I totally know how to play this" vibes (spoiler: I don't).

Then comes the inevitable interruption. "Beautiful sunset, huh?" Priyanka's voice cut through my deep, totally-not-pretentious thoughts.

I turned to see her and Koushik, hand in hand, like they were straight out of some Instagram couple goals page. Cute. But also, yeah, whatever.

"Yeah," I replied, looking back at the sun, trying to hold onto my dramatic moment. I fished out my cigarette pack and offered one to Koushik, the guy who's been my partner-in-crime since college. You know the kind—the friend who has all your embarrassing stories but still acts like an adult while you're stuck pretending life's a sitcom.

Wait, am I rambling? Yeah, I do that. You'll get used to it. Anyway, back to the story.

There we were, soaking in the golden glow of the sunset, talking about life, college, and how we're all *definitely* going to be responsible adults someday. Or not.

"You down for a trip to Kaziranga?" Koushik asked, mid-cigarette drag.

"Who's going?" I asked, already sensing the inevitable couple-filled disaster.

"James, Joya, Pranab, Silpi... the gang."

Right. The *gang*—aka, the collective of couples I'd third-wheel so hard I might as well have been a spare tire. "Nah, I'll pass," I said. "You guys will be off having cute couple moments, and I'll be sitting in a corner with a beer and a cigarette, contemplating life. I can do that from here, minus the travel."

Efficiently antisocial, that's me. Priyanka headed inside to raid my kitchen (standard procedure), and Koushik and I migrated to my mini bar. Whiskey for him, another coffee for me, because apparently I was feeling rebellious in a caffeine kind of way.

Fast forward: we're lounging around, reminiscing about college, while the sun dips below the horizon like it's trying to upstage our nostalgia. By now, you might be wondering, "Why all the sunset talk?" Well, trust me—this sunset is going to matter later. No spoilers, though. Keep your popcorn ready.

For the record, I'm not a chain-smoking, whiskey-chugging recluse. I just happen to have a Sunday-to-Monday smoking rule. You know, to keep things balanced.

Anyway, life went on in its usual way: work and smoke breaks. Then, one evening, the universe decided to get cute. Picture me, cruising through the city on my bike at dusk—cue cinematic background music. Instagram had been raving about this new café, *Nerds* (and no, they're not paying me to drop their name, but they should). So, naturally, I decided to check it out.

I walk in, find a cozy corner, and that's when it happens. *The moment.*

I see her.

Now, I know what you're thinking: "Oh great, here comes the cheesy 'love at first sight' moment." And you know what? You're not wrong. But there was something about her—sitting there, lost in her book, glasses perched on her nose, hair falling over her face like she'd just stepped out of some Netflix rom-com. A coffee cup sat beside her, but she was way more into the book than her pasta. Classic.

Here's where I should probably describe the book, but let's be real—no one cares, and I'm not getting paid for product placements. So let's skip that.

All I could think was, *Wow.* Yeah, I know. Not exactly Shakespeare, but when you're hit by a wave of feelings that you haven't prepared for, eloquence isn't exactly top of mind.

Before I could even process the "crush symptoms" in full, she got up, collected her things, and disappeared into a cab. And just like that, she was gone. So, naturally, I did the only thing a rational person would do—I walked to the café's smoking area, lit another cigarette, and tried to figure out what just happened.

Now, I get it. You're probably rolling your eyes. "Oh, great, here's another guy who thinks he's in a rom-com." But hold on! Fate has a sense of humor, and this story isn't done playing out.

Days passed. I did the usual—work, dating apps (because yeah, I was that guy), and no sign of her anywhere. But the universe? Oh, it wasn't done with me yet.

Note from the writer*: Gaurav's a slow burn, folks. We're just setting the stage here. But if you're thinking "Oh no, another guy who thinks a glance is true love," hold tight. The real fun hasn't even started yet. This is just a warm-up. You know the drill: boy sees girl, boy overthinks, boy tries not to embarrass himself. Stay tuned.*

1

Fate Rides Pillion

A few days later, I woke up to the obnoxious sound of my iPhone alarm. (Apple, if you're reading this, I'm open to sponsorship. Just saying.) It was 4 AM, an ungodly hour to be awake, but there I was, sipping coffee and starting up my pride and joy—my Royal Enfield Continental GT 650. Yep, it's loud, it's beautiful, and it was a graduation gift from my dad. (Still not sponsored. I'll stop now.)

By 7 AM, I arrived at the meetup point. Everyone was already there, because of course they were.

"You actually came!" Aditya greeted me with a smirk.

"Like I'd miss this?" I shot back sarcastically.

Bornali chimed in, looking relieved. "Thank God you didn't bail. We had a little issue."

"Yeah? What kind of issue?"

"Well, Aradhya was supposed to come, but she canceled last minute. And Prakriti—who was Aradhya's pillion—is already here. So, um, I told her she could ride with you."

Wait—what now?

I turned around just as I heard a soft voice behind me. "Hi."

And guess what? It was her. *The* girl from the café. Standing there, right in front of me. I swear my heart did a backflip.

"Uh... hi, I'm Gaurav," I said, trying to sound like I hadn't been weirdly obsessed with finding her for weeks. Confidence on the outside, absolute chaos on the inside.

"Prakriti," she replied with a smile that could probably melt glaciers.

What are the odds, right? The universe, I tell you, it has a wicked sense of humor.

And before I knew it, she was climbing onto the back of my bike. My brain was screaming, *This can't be real!*

We started cruising along NH 715, the road cutting through the lush green forests. It was perfect. The weather, the vibe, her.

"You okay back there?" I asked, trying to sound casual.

"Yeah, I'm good," she replied.

The conversation was small, but my mind was racing. Here I was, riding through one of the most beautiful places on earth, with the girl I'd been thinking about for days sitting behind me. And yeah, my stomach was doing those weird butterfly things again.

So, that's how it all started. If you're still with me, congrats. The ride is just beginning. Literally.

So there we were. Me, her, and the open road. Honestly, if my life were a Netflix show, this would be the part where they'd cue some epic indie music—probably something by The Lumineers or Mumford & Sons. Maybe throw in a slow-motion shot of us driving through the mist, hair blowing in the wind, looking effortlessly cool. Spoiler: in real life, my helmet made me look like a bobblehead, and there was no wind blowing majestically through anyone's hair.

But hey, this is *my* story, so let's pretend it looked cinematic.

We sped down NH 715, winding through lush green forests and tea gardens, and for the first time in weeks, I wasn't obsessing over whether or not I'd left the stove on back home. Nope, my mind was entirely occupied by the girl sitting behind me. Prakriti. Yeah, I know, it sounds like a name plucked straight from an art-house film. *This girl*—the same one I'd been dreaming about since that day in the café—was now on my bike, with her arms gently wrapped around my waist. Casual, no big deal. Except my brain was freaking out like a cat seeing a cucumber for the first time.

I'd love to say something deep and meaningful was running through my mind—like the nature of fate, or how we're all just tiny specs in a vast, indifferent universe. But honestly? My brain was like, "Holy crap, is this happening? Don't mess this up, Gaurav."

At this point, you're probably thinking, "Dude, calm down, it's just a road trip." And you'd be right. Except it wasn't just a road trip. It was *the* road trip. The kind that only happens once in a lifetime—unless you're a rom-com protagonist, then it happens at least twice, with a dramatic breakup in between. But I digress.

After a while, we pulled over at a roadside tea stall—because road trips in Assam without tea are basically illegal. (No, seriously. Look it up. You won't find anything, but trust me on this one.)

I ordered two cups of chai and handed one to her. The moment she took it, I felt this weird surge of excitement. Like, oh wow, I just gave her tea. Yeah, I know. I'm a romantic disaster.

"You're quiet," she said, her voice gentle but with just enough curiosity to keep me from awkwardly disappearing into my chai cup. "Is that normal for you, or should I be concerned?"

Oh boy. We're doing this now? Okay, Gaurav, time to turn on the charm—or at least the part of my brain that knows how to string together words without sounding like an idiot.

"Just mentally preparing for the inevitable embarrassment that comes with me being me," I replied with a smirk. *Nailed it.* Well, in my head I did. She smiled though, so that's a win.

"Is that your thing? Self-deprecation?" she asked, sipping her tea.

"Pretty much. That, and avoiding small talk." I took a sip too, pretending that I wasn't already thinking about ways to prolong this conversation. *Maybe I should ask about her hobbies? No, too generic. What's her favorite conspiracy theory? Too weird. Focus, Gaurav!*

"What about you?" I asked, shifting gears before I spiraled into my own overthinking. "Are you always this mysterious, or is this just an act for the bike rides?"

She laughed—a soft, genuine laugh that made my stomach do that stupid flippy thing again. "I don't know. Maybe I'm just trying to figure you out. You don't seem like the usual 'biker guy' stereotype."

"Oh, I'm definitely not," I said. "I'm the guy who googles 'how to look cool on a bike' the night before a ride."

And there it was—the laugh again. I was starting to feel like I might not completely screw this up after all.

Now, if this were a perfect rom-com, the rest of the trip would've been smooth sailing. Maybe some light banter, a cute moment where our hands accidentally touched, and by the end of the day, we'd both be ready to exchange dramatic declarations of love under the setting sun. But no. Life, dear reader, has a twisted sense of humor.

So, there we were, back on the road after our chai stop, the wind whipping past us as we made our way through the scenic countryside. I was starting to feel pretty good about myself—maybe even a little *too* good. You know when things are going so well that you just know something's about to go wrong? Yeah, it was that moment.

We were cruising along, everything was perfect, and then—boom. Out of nowhere, a giant pothole. The kind that looks like it's secretly trying to swallow your bike whole and spit you out in another dimension. In the fraction of a second, I did what any *experienced* biker would do: I panicked.

I swerved, my heart leaping into my throat. The bike wobbled like a drunk toddler on a pogo stick, and I could hear Prakriti let out a surprised *"Whoa!"* from behind me. I was *this* close to sending us both flying into a ditch.

"Sorry!" I yelled over the engine, my face heating up with embarrassment. "Wasn't expecting that!"

Prakriti, to her credit, didn't scream or freak out. Instead, she just tightened her grip on me and said, "It's fine! Just... watch out for those road traps."

At this point, I'd like to remind you, dear reader, that I'm *not* a professional rider. I'm just a guy with a bike and a growing sense of dread that maybe, just maybe, I wasn't as cool as I thought I was. *Wait, did I ever think I was cool? No? Okay, moving on.*

After that near-death experience, I pulled over to take a breather. The bike was fine, I was fine, and more importantly—Prakriti hadn't decided to abandon me in the middle of nowhere. Small victories, folks.

We sat on the side of the road, overlooking a wide field with nothing but green for miles. It was quiet. Peaceful. And just awkward enough that I had to say something before the silence swallowed us both whole.

"Hey, so, I gotta ask..." I started, staring at the horizon, trying to look casual. "Why'd you agree to come on this trip?"

Prakriti raised an eyebrow. "Why wouldn't I? I mean, it's not every day I get to ride through Kaziranga with a total stranger who almost dumps us into a pothole the size of Mars."

"Fair point." I laughed, though inwardly I was cringing. *Way to bring up the pothole again, Gaurav.*

"No, but seriously," she continued, her voice softer now. "I guess I needed a break from things. Life's been a little... I don't know, overwhelming lately. This trip seemed like a good escape."

"Yeah, I get that," I said, nodding. "Life's kinda like one long series of potholes, isn't it?"

She gave me a look. "Did you just compare life to a pothole?"

"Well, yeah. I mean, think about it. You're cruising along, everything's fine, and then—boom. Out of nowhere, something messes up your day. But you swerve, try to recover, and keep going."

"Interesting metaphor." She smiled, and for a second, I felt like maybe I wasn't completely hopeless at this.

We sat there for a while, watching the sun start its slow descent toward the horizon. And as cheesy as it sounds (yes, I'm self-aware), there was something nice about the silence. Like maybe we didn't need to fill it with endless chatter.

Of course, just as I was about to bask in the moment and maybe work up the courage to ask her something deeper, she broke the silence.

"So... how many times have you actually dropped your bike?" she asked, a mischievous glint in her eye.

And there it was. The charm of the universe, once again reminding me not to take myself too seriously.

"Only once. Maybe twice," I admitted with a grin. "But don't worry. I've got this under control."

She laughed, and just like that, the tension melted away. Turns out, nearly crashing your bike can actually be a decent icebreaker. Who knew?

So, there you have it. That's how our little road trip began—awkward, a little dangerous, and filled with enough pothole metaphors to last a lifetime. But if you think that's the end of the story, think again. We've only just scratched the surface.

Because here's the thing about life: it's messy. It's unpredictable. And sometimes, it throws the right people in your path (or on your bike) when you least expect it. The universe? It's got jokes. But every now and then, those jokes lead to something real.

And trust me, dear reader, this is only the beginning. Buckle up. The ride'

Note form the writer: *So, Gaurav finally got the girl... sort of. But did you really think the universe was going to let him off that easily? Nope. Not a chance. Also, if you're wondering, yes, Gaurav is that guy—overthinking while nearly dumping them both into a pothole. What did I tell you? Never a dull moment when the universe is your co-pilot, and it's been reading way too many rom-coms.*

Stay tuned. There's bound to be another metaphor... and probably another near-disaster.

2
The Accidental Like

So, after spending what can only be described as one of the best days of my life (and trust me, I'm not prone to hyperbole—except when I am), we headed back. You know how people always say, "I'll never forget this day"? Well, for once, I actually believe it. The breeze, the laughter, the feeling that life was just a little bit lighter with her around—it was all there, locked in my mental vault of perfect moments.

And yes, Prakriti was as cute as ever. *Cue the heart eyes emoji.* You know that thing that happens when you're falling for someone? The stomach flips, the random smiles, and the over-analyzing every word they say? Yeah, I was living that cliché, and I wasn't even mad about it. You get me, right? You've probably been there. And if you haven't, well, buckle up, friend. It's one heck of a ride.

After dropping her off, I headed home, back to my not-so-dramatic life, where I was greeted by Hardy. Oh, I almost forgot to introduce him to you properly. Everyone, meet Hardy. Hardy, say hello to the readers! Yeah, that's right, he doesn't say much. But don't be fooled by the tiny little guy—he's a stone-cold serial killer.

Hardy is my pet turtle, and let me tell you, he's always hungry. I have no idea how he fits so much food in that miniature shell of his. Like, seriously, I feed him every day, and he just keeps munching away, probably plotting his next move. Oh, and did I mention? Hardy's got a *dark side.* He's responsible for the tragic demise of two of my pet goldfish. *RIP, Goldy and Flash.* I guess the whole "slow and steady" thing really paid off for Hardy, but for the goldfish, not so much.

Anyway, I fed him—mostly to keep him from taking out any more aquatic hit jobs—and settled into the couch, ready for a low-key evening. That's when I made the *big* mistake. You know the one. We've all been there: it's called Instagram.

Now, I don't know what it is about Instagram, but it turns perfectly rational people into professional-grade stalkers. One minute, you're casually scrolling through your feed, the next, you're deep-diving into someone's photos from three years ago like you're Indiana Jones hunting for ancient treasures.

So there I was, phone in hand, heart still doing its post-Prakriti dance, when I decided to do the obvious thing: I searched her up. You know, just to see if she had any new posts, or stories, or... I don't know, maybe a selfie with a caption that was suspiciously about a guy who rides bikes and almost crashes into potholes?

A quick search, and boom—there she was. *Prakriti.* Profile picture? Adorable. Followers? Way more than I could ever hope to have. Bio? Minimalist but classy. I hit the follow button, my heart beating just a little faster, and then casually—okay, not so casually—began scrolling through her profile.

Now, let's be clear. I was *just* looking. Harmless curiosity, right? It's not like I was obsessing over every detail of her life. Just, you know, getting a sense of her vibe. The usual.

And then... it happened.

Bam! I don't know how or why, but I liked one of her old photos. Not recent. No, no. That would've been too easy. We're talking a two-year-old photo. Two. Freaking. Years. And not just any photo—one where she was wearing this ridiculously cute winter hat, holding a cup of hot chocolate. The kind of photo that screams, "I'm adorable, and now you're screwed."

I froze. Time stopped. My brain went into meltdown mode. *Did I really just do that?*

Yes. Yes, I did.

Cue the internal screaming. My thumb, in all its clumsy glory, had betrayed me. *Stalking King* in the house, everyone. Round of applause for the new achievement unlocked: Liking a two-year-old photo on Instagram. Just kill me now.

Now, if you've ever been in this situation, you know there's only one thing to do: *unlike* the photo. Delete the evidence. Act like nothing happened. Simple, right?

But here's the thing: The damage had been done. My panic-fueled finger did the job, but Instagram had already sent out its betrayal. Prakriti would now know. She would *see* that I had scrolled through years of her life like some kind of Instagram detective. And that little heart icon? It would now glow like a neon sign saying, "Yep, I'm that guy."

I quickly unliked it, but who was I kidding? She probably already got the notification. *Smooth move, Gaurav. Real smooth.*

At this point, I was pacing around my living room, half-expecting a message from her asking, "Why were you creeping on my profile?" Or worse—complete silence, forever branded as the guy who couldn't handle a simple follow without messing it up.

In my mind, I could see Hardy staring up at me from his tank, judging me with his cold, reptilian eyes. *You fool*, he seemed to say. *You let your thumb do the thinking.*

"Shut up, Hardy," I muttered, as if a turtle with homicidal tendencies could understand my shame.

And then... nothing. No messages, no calls. Just me, sitting there in my own anxiety stew, waiting for some kind of response—anything that would either confirm or, in a miracle scenario, dismiss my epic Instagram fail.

I mean, I could have just played it cool. Pretended it was an accidental like (which, technically, it was), and let it go. But nope. Instead, I spent the next hour overthinking my entire life, all thanks to a single tap on a two-year-old photo.

Pro tip: If you ever find yourself in this situation, close the app, put the phone down, and walk away. Trust me. Nothing good ever comes from trying to fix things after an Instagram deep dive gone wrong.

And thus, dear reader, ended one of the most *tragic* social media moments of my life. But hey, if there's one thing I've learned from this whole experience, it's that I'm not exactly the smoothest guy in the world. And you know what? I'm okay with that. Sort of.

So there you have it—my day with Prakriti ended on a high note, only to be followed by a self-inflicted Instagram disaster. But this is far from over. Because one thing's for sure: fate, the universe, or whatever cosmic force that brought us together on that bike trip? Yeah, it's not done with us yet.

Stay tuned, dear reader. This ride is just getting started.

3

Turtle-Sanctioned Chaos

Feeding the overly excitable Hardy—who was currently attempting to steal my toothbrush like it was some prized trophy—set the tone for my morning. Seriously, if this turtle had any more energy, I'd be considering a career in turtle Olympics.

As I wrestled my toothbrush free, I opened Instagram and saw that Prakriti had followed me back! Oh, and she tagged me in her story about yesterday's ride. You know the feeling, right? It's like the universe just handed you a trophy for being a lovable goof. My heart did a backflip while my stomach fluttered like a confused butterfly.

Naturally, I re-posted her story with all the enthusiasm of a kid in a candy store. "Look, everyone! My crush noticed me! How do I make this less awkward?!"

I proceeded to make breakfast, balancing a cigarette in one hand while attempting to channel my inner chef. The menu? Black coffee, some perfectly toasted bread, and a single egg—because nothing says "I'm an adult" like a sad, solitary egg.

Now, what do I do for a living, you ask? I'm a Software Developer which, as far as jobs go, is about as exciting as watching paint dry. Thanks to our benevolent CEO, most of us IT folks get to work from home in our pajamas, which, let's be honest, is a blessing and a curse. I mean, who else can confidently say they've attended a meeting in their boxers while drinking coffee straight from the pot?

And then there's Hardy, who is probably judging my life choices while basking in the sunlight. "Really, Gaurav? This is your career? You could've been a professional napper, you know."

As I sipped my coffee—okay, inhaled it—I liked Prakriti's story and texted her: "It was a really wonderful day with you."

And then, the dreaded typing dots appeared. You know those dots, right? They're the modern equivalent of waiting for a pot to boil. The suspense was unbearable. "C'mon, Prakriti, don't leave me hanging here!"

Finally, she replied: "Yes, it was really a break from the hassle. I really needed that."

Suddenly, my mind went blank. What do I say now? "So, what's your favorite kind of cheese?" Not exactly the smoothest transition from "we had a great time" to "please marry me."

Just as I was about to brainstorm a witty reply, my phone flashed another message: "Catch you later; I have some work to do." Ah, the classic brush-off. I sent back an "Okay" emoji that screamed, "I'm totally cool with this!" even though I felt like a deflated balloon.

And now we return to real life, where I was left in a state of utter confusion. The time with her yesterday had flown by like a bad rom-com. Why couldn't I think of anything else to say? I mean, it's not like I was trying to solve world hunger here.

Note from the writer: *If you're wondering what happened to Gaurav's friends, don't worry! They're just plot devices designed to create chaos and help our dear Gaurav realize that he has a love life to figure out. Fictional characters need friends too, right? Think of them as my way of spicing things up—kind of like adding extra cheese to a pizza when you're already fully aware of your lactose intolerance. Enjoy the story; I may pop in again to guide you through this delightful mess of emotions.*

And with that, I went back to staring at my phone, contemplating if I could master the courage to ask Prakriti out—because let's face it, every rom-com needs a bit of awkwardness.

So, the day rolled by in its usual fashion—work, procrastination, and a few stolen moments imagining how this new chapter might unfold. By evening, I couldn't shake the thought of texting Prakriti. You know that feeling when you overthink every single word, like you're suddenly a diplomat negotiating world peace? Yeah, that was me.

I typed out, "What are your plans for the rest of the day?" then stared at it like it was a Shakespearean sonnet. "Rest of the day" sounded a bit... formal, like I was her boss checking in on her weekend schedule. So, naturally, I edited and re-edited like a man on a mission.

Note from the writer: *If you've ever obsessively rephrased a text to a crush, congratulations, you're in the club. It's a universal rite of passage.*

Eventually, I sent what I thought was the most harmless, casual text ever crafted in the history of human communication: **"Hey, what's your plan tonight?"** Sent. Delivered. Anxiety in full gear. And then—buzz! A reply popped up almost instantly: **"Nothing much, just binge-watching some pending series."**

Okay, I thought. Here's my chance. In my head, I'm already running a mental marathon, debating whether to ask her out for coffee, or just leave her to her Netflix marathon. **Hardy**, my wise turtle companion, wasn't much help. He just blinked, as if saying, "Dude, you've got this. Or you don't. I don't know, I'm a turtle."

"Alright, here goes nothing," I mumbled to myself and typed: **"Let's have a cup of coffee at some café?"**

The second I hit send, it felt like my heart paused mid-beat. You know that feeling when you send a risky text, and you want to throw your phone out the window to avoid seeing the reply? Yeah, that was me. I looked at Hardy again. "Seriously, man, you're supposed to be my emotional support turtle here. Help me out!" Hardy, ever the calm one, just stared like I was being dramatic. Which I was.

Then—**buzz!** Her reply came in: **"Okay, 7:30 PM, pick me up near Mission Chariali."**

Wait, what? **Did I just get a green signal?** I looked at my phone, then at Hardy. "Did that just happen?!" Hardy, bless his turtle heart, blinked again as if to say, "It's not a dream, dude. Get your act together."

Cue the mini victory dance. My heart was practically doing somersaults, and I couldn't stop grinning like an idiot. **An unofficial date.** With **Prakriti.** My crush. Is this what cloud nine feels like?

Note from the writer:*If you're sitting there thinking, "Wow, Gaurav's losing it over coffee," you're absolutely right. This is what happens when you've got a turtle as your only roommate for too long.*

Now, the real challenge begins. What to wear, how to act, and most importantly, how not to say anything incredibly awkward when I pick her up.

So, there I was, pacing around my room, mentally rehearsing the perfect way to pick her up. **"Hey, how's it going?"** No, too casual. **"Hey! You look amazing!"** Wait, too much. Maybe I should go with something simple: **"Hi."** Yeah, simple works, right? Then I started running through all the questions I could ask her to keep the conversation flowing. You know, the classic "What's your favorite movie?" or "Do you like turtles?" You can never go wrong with turtles. Hardy agrees.

Honestly, preparing for this first unofficial date felt like I was prepping for some high-stakes diplomatic meeting. My brain was going full-speed, imagining every possible scenario, planning out the smoothest responses, and timing the perfect jokes.

Note from the writer*: If you think rehearsing for a date is overkill, well...you've never met **me**.*

I paused for a second, looked at Hardy, and sighed. "You know, if I spent this much effort on my actual job, I'd probably be CEO by now." Hardy, of course, didn't care. He just blinked lazily from his tank, his face saying, "You're lucky if you can even get out of this without tripping over yourself."

Now, back to reality. I needed to dress the part. Not too fancy, but also not "I just woke up and grabbed the first thing I saw." The problem? Every single piece of clothing I owned was black. Like, **seriously**, my wardrobe looked like Batman had taken over. Black t-shirts, black jeans, black shoes—everything screamed "I'm too cool for color," or maybe just "I'm lazy and don't want to think about what to wear."

"Great, Gaurav," I muttered to myself, "you're going on an unofficial date, not a funeral."

But let's be honest: black is a safe choice. It's my uniform, my go-to. It's basically the same strategy millionaires use with their wardrobes. Less decision-making, more focus. Hardy, from his tank, seemed unimpressed by my pseudo-philosophy. His expression was clearly, "Dude, you're not a millionaire. Get over it."

"Okay, fine, you're right," I said, staring at my reflection in the mirror. "I'm not here for a fashion parade. I'm going to meet Prakriti, and that's all that matters."

Now, while I may not have a colorful wardrobe, there was one area I **did** excel in—perfume. I had an entire shelf dedicated to colognes and scents. If my clothes couldn't make a statement, my fragrance would. This was the moment I'd been waiting for. I scanned my collection, carefully selecting the absolute best of the best. Something that says, **'I'm interesting,'** but not **'I'm trying too hard.'** Something that gives me the vibe of a guy who's confident...but also not a millionaire. Hardy seemed to approve.

4

The Batmobile, A Daisy, and A Date

❤

I was officially in the Batmobile, or rather, my trusty Continental GT 650, dressed head to toe in black. Yep, I basically looked like I was auditioning for the next Batman movie. Only difference? Batman saves Gotham; I'm here just trying not to mess up a first date. Oh, and in case you're wondering, no, my heart's not black—just everything else I own is.

The road was calm as I cruised towards the pick-up spot, heart racing faster than my bike, but I made it early (better to be the early bird than the awkwardly late one, right?). After a few minutes, I saw her, and man, did she look like she just walked out of a movie scene—hair flowing, red lipstick perfectly applied, and that white dress... I swear I forgot how to breathe for a second. She was dazzling, and there I was, trying to play it cool in my all-black "I-hope-she-doesn't-think-my-soul-is-dark" attire.

As she walked closer, I mentally rehearsed what I had planned. **"Hi, how's it going?"** But instead, all I could manage was a wave and what was probably the world's most awkward smile. And then came the anxiety bomb.

I had a plan, you see. I didn't want to show up empty-handed. I had bought her a flower—well, technically, a yellow daisy, because roses felt too much for a first "unofficial" date. But then I panicked and taped the daisy to a chocolate bar because... why not? It seemed like a genius idea at the time. Now, I was questioning my life decisions. **What if she thinks this is weird? What if I'm moving too fast?**

And then, she smiled. That smile could power a small city, I'm telling you.

"Hi," she said, her voice as sweet as it was calming. I handed her the daisy-chocolate combo with all the grace of someone about to pass out from anxiety.

"For you," I muttered, pretty sure I was shaking a little. My anxiety level? Through the roof. I could take on an army of rhinos with my bare hands right now, or... you know, just completely pass out if she rejected the flower.

But she took it, and guess what? Her cheeks turned red. **She was blushing!** "Thank you so much," she said, her smile getting even brighter. At this point, I had no idea what to do with myself. **Success! I didn't blow it!**

I motioned to my bike. "Hop on," I said, trying to sound casual, but my heart was probably running laps inside my chest.

We started rolling, the engine purring under us, and for a while, neither of us said anything. It wasn't awkward though. It was one of those rare, peaceful silences, where even with the noise of the city around us, it felt like we were in our own little bubble. It was calm. I was calm. For once, I wasn't overthinking everything, just... existing in the moment.

Then I realized I should probably break the silence before it got *too* long. "So... where do we head now?" I asked, pretending I didn't have about five different café options already mapped out in my head.

She gave me this calm, sweet smile and said, "You decide. I'm comfortable wherever you take me."

No pressure, right?

***Note from the writer**:Look, if you're sitting there thinking **"Why's Gaurav so nervous?"**—well, let me ask you this: How often do you go on an unofficial first date with your crush? Exactly. It's nerve-wracking stuff! And if you're wondering about the daisy-chocolate combo, well, let's just call that Gaurav's unique brand of charm. But hey, that's what makes these moments memorable, right? You stumble, you fumble, and somehow, it all turns out okay. Or maybe not. You'll have to keep reading to find out whether Gaurav keeps his cool or if Hardy, the overconfident turtle, gives him better advice next time.*

That word really just melted down my heart... she's comfortable wherever I take her." Seriously, what is this? A rom-com or the beginning of a feel-good ad for heartwarming friendships? Either way, I was in deep. I had a fancy café in mind—no spoilers on the name, but trust me, I knew Prakriti would fall in love with its vibe.

We pulled up, and I held the door for her like a gentleman. "After you," I said, trying not to sound too awkward.

She smiled and said, "Thank you." It was one of those smiles that hits you right in the chest.

We picked a table by the window. Now, don't get me wrong, I wasn't about to go full-on "romantic hero" and pull out her chair—I mean, there's smooth, and then there's *too much*, right?

"So, have you been here before?" I asked, trying to keep the conversation flowing.

She shook her head, smiling. "No, I haven't. Have you?"

"Yeah, it's pretty popular. Won an award last year for the best café in town."

Now, let's pause for a second. There's this soft piano music playing, the lighting is just right, and everything looks perfect. But you know what really ties this whole scene together? Prakriti. I swear I'm not being too cheesy (okay, maybe a little), but she just fit perfectly into this moment. But hey, if I'm coming off as cringe in my narration, cut me some slack—this is real life, not a scripted scene.

"So, you have a turtle, right? He's really cute," she said, out of nowhere. A big shout-out to Hardy for saving me here.

"Yeah, that's Hardy! He's the real boss at home," I said, feeling a little proud. Hardy was getting the attention he deserved.

"He's adorable," she added.

I nodded, but curiosity got the better of me. "So, what brings you to Tezpur?"

"I'm a freelance writer. Just finished my Masters at Tezpur University."

"That's amazing!" I said, genuinely impressed. She was both smart and creative—this girl was something else.

"What about you?" she asked, just as the waiter arrived. We ordered two coffees—classic—and I went for a club sandwich while she picked momos. Turns out, momos are her favorite. I mentally filed that away for future reference.

"I'm a software developer," I replied, jumping back into our Q&A session. Things were moving smoothly, and I was sticking to the script I'd mentally rehearsed. All those nerves from earlier? They were starting to fade.

"Wow, tech guy huh?" she said with a playful smirk. I smiled, showing way too much tooth, trying to play it cool. At this point, everything was calculated—every sip of water, every neck movement, even the rhythm of my breathing. I was doing everything in slow motion, like some ultra-composed action hero. But then, *boom*, she hit me with an out-of-syllabus question.

"Gaurav, apart from coding and Hardy, do you have someone special?" she asked, raising her eyebrows like she just pulled a joker card.

I felt like I'd just been hit with a pop quiz I hadn't studied for. "Like... my parents?" I said, playing dumb like it was some genius defense strategy.

"No, I know you love them," she replied, still smiling. "I mean... do you have a girlfriend?"

And there it was. The question that could be interpreted in *so* many different ways. The pressure in the room shot up as if Hardy himself had just turned the heat up a notch.

"Currently, I'm single," I said carefully, weighing every word like I was coding a delicate program. "But yeah, once upon a time, a girl broke my heart." I ended it with a hint of drama, you know, just to keep things interesting.

Her smile faded slightly, replaced with a more thoughtful look. "Do you miss her?" she asked, tilting her head just enough to make it feel like a loaded question.

"Nah," I said, shaking my head. "The relationship didn't even last a year. We were just too different, and it's been like three years now." I felt like I was navigating a minefield with that answer, trying to be honest without sounding bitter or too detached. Did I handle it well? I guess only she could tell.

And because I didn't want to be the only one sweating, I fired the question back at her. "What about you?"

I had no idea if that was the right move or not. This was definitely one of those out-of-syllabus topics you don't prep for when you're mentally rehearsing for a date. The ball was in her court now, and I wasn't sure if I was ready for her answer.

Prakriti smiled warmly after I tossed the question back to her, a twinkle in her eyes as she leaned back into her chair. "Oh, you're trying to turn the tables on me now, huh?" she teased, and I couldn't help but grin, feeling a mixture of relief and curiosity.

"Well, it's only fair," I said, trying to keep my voice casual but definitely not as smooth as I intended.

She took a small sip of her coffee before answering. "I've had my share of relationships, yes," she began, her voice soft, reflective. "There was someone in college. We dated for a while, but it fizzled out. No drama or anything, just... life pulling us in different directions, I guess."

I nodded, feeling the relief settle in knowing it wasn't something too heavy. "I think that's how a lot of relationships end. No big breakups, just people growing apart."

"Yeah, exactly," she said, and for a moment, her gaze drifted out of the café window as if replaying those memories. "But I guess it wasn't meant to be, and I'm okay with that."

There was a brief pause as the waiter brought our order—her plate of steaming momos and my sandwich. The aroma was comforting, and I felt like we were slowly easing into a more comfortable rhythm.

I decided to lighten things up. "So, momos are your favorite dish, huh? I guess I'll have to become an expert at cooking them if I want to impress you."

She laughed, covering her mouth with her hand in the cutest way. "Oh, you cook? That's already impressive! Most guys I know can barely manage toast."

I shrugged with exaggerated modesty. "Well, toast is my specialty, but I'm open to learning the art of momo-making for the right person." I shot her a playful look, hoping to keep the conversation light and fun.

Prakriti raised her eyebrows, clearly entertained by my attempt at humor. "Okay, let's see—next time, I expect homemade momos."

"Challenge accepted," I said, though my mind was already trying to figure out how the hell I was going to learn to make momos without completely embarrassing myself. Maybe YouTube tutorials could save me from future disaster.

As we ate, the conversation flowed naturally. We talked about everything from our favorite TV shows to places we'd love to travel, and I found out that she's a big fan of mystery novels, which was kind of funny because, well, she was a mystery to me up until this evening.

"So, Tezpur, huh?" I asked between bites of my sandwich. "Is it just the freelancing that brought you here, or do you have roots here?"

"I grew up here, actually," she said, dabbing her lips with a napkin. "But I was away for a while—college, work, the usual. I only recently came back. There's something about this place, you know? As much as I wanted to get away, it feels like home."

"Yeah, I get that," I said, even though Tezpur was still a bit unfamiliar to me. But there was something about her passion for the place that made me see it in a new light. Maybe it wasn't so much about where we were, but who we were with.

The conversation drifted into comfortable silence again. She was playing with the edge of her coffee cup, and I was trying to think of a smooth segue into the next topic. I didn't want the date to end. I liked being around her, and the thought of parting ways too soon felt... off.

But before I could come up with another topic, Prakriti glanced at me with a mischievous grin. "So, Mr. Software Developer, what's your big dream? Like, if you weren't coding away, what would you be doing?"

Ah, this was a good one. I didn't have to think long for an answer. "I'd be a full-time traveler, hopping from country to country with my bike and Hardy in tow. Just us, the open road, and... maybe some momos along the way," I said with a wink.

She burst out laughing, the sound warm and full of life. "Hardy on the road trip? I'd pay to see that. He'd have his own little helmet!"

"Exactly! Hardy would be the coolest turtle on the planet. People would stop us just to take pictures with him," I joked, feeling more relaxed by the second.

We finished our food, the evening growing darker outside, and yet it felt like things were just beginning between us. There was an energy in the air—a shared excitement, but also something comfortable, like we'd known each other longer than just a couple of meet-ups.

I paid the bill, and as we stepped outside, the air was cooler now, the night embracing us in its quiet. "So, what next?" I asked her, half-hoping she'd say she didn't want the night to end either.

She looked at me, her eyes gleaming. "How about a walk? We could check out the riverside."

I smiled. "Perfect."

We hopped on my bike again—the *black* Continental GT 650, because yes, apparently, I have a theme—and headed towards the riverside. The cool breeze hit my face, and for once, I wasn't overthinking everything. Well, okay, I was. I'm still calculating which side of the road makes me look more heroic in case of a spontaneous slow-motion movie scene. You know, just in case.

As we arrived, we parked and started walking along the riverbank. It was quiet, peaceful, and for a second, it felt like we were the only two people in the universe. And here's where I'll break the fourth wall—don't worry, I'm fully aware that's super cheesy. But hey, if I don't romanticize this moment now, future me will be like, "Dude, you missed your chance to sound deep and profound."

"So," I said, breaking the silence, "What's your take on this whole unofficial date? Rate it on a scale of 'awkward silence' to 'second date potential'."

Prakriti smirked, clearly entertained by my question. "Well, Hardy definitely earns you bonus points."

"Hardy does have that effect," I nodded seriously, feeling a silent thank-you owed to the little guy back home.

She giggled again, and it was one of those moments where everything felt light. But then—oh, here comes the curveball. "You're not as awkward as I expected, Gaurav," she said, playfully bumping my shoulder.

Now, I have to pause the story for a second. You see, dear reader, this is what you call a *left-handed compliment.* It's like saying, "Hey, you don't suck as much as I thought you would!" What do I even do with that?

I quickly recovered. "Thanks, I try not to be a complete disaster in public."

She grinned, and we kept walking in sync. "To be honest," she started, looking out at the river, "I'm glad you asked me out. I wasn't sure if we'd vibe, but tonight's been... fun."

I don't want to say my heart did a somersault, but let's just say it *definitely* skipped a beat. And no, not in the "I should see a doctor" kind of way.

I kept it cool, though. "Well, I've been trying to impress you all night. Hardy's not the only one working hard here."

Prakriti chuckled again, and we continued walking along the river, side by side, the conversation flowing naturally now. No more rehearsals, no more calculations—just the two of us in the moment. Well, okay, maybe a *few* calculations, like when to bring up another joke and make sure she doesn't think my heart is as black as my wardrobe.

Note from the writer:*Okay, let's pause for a sec. You're probably thinking, "This is going way too smoothly, right?" And yes, you're correct. In any decent story, something has to go wrong—like maybe I step in a puddle, or Hardy somehow texts me that he's planning a jailbreak from the tank. But for now, we'll let Gaurav have this win. He deserves it after all that pre-date panic. But stay tuned, things are bound to get messy. Because, you know, life.*

As we kept walking along the river, the lights from the distant buildings reflected on the water, creating a shimmering effect. It was quiet, but the good kind of quiet—like the world was giving us space to figure out whatever this was.

"So, what's the story with your whole 'all-black-everything' vibe?" Prakriti asked, eyeing my attire as we strolled. "You some kind of undercover superhero I should know about?"

I laughed. "If I told you, I'd have to erase your memory. Standard superhero rules."

She raised an eyebrow, amused. "Oh really? So, what's your superhero name? *Captain Blackout?*"

"More like *The Midnight Coder*," I grinned, "Fighting bugs by day, sipping coffee by night."

Prakriti giggled, and that sound—it was like the perfect tune, you know? And okay, I'm getting corny again. But seriously, it felt good to make her laugh.

I looked around and spotted a bench facing the river. "Wanna sit for a bit?" I asked.

She nodded, and we both sat down, the cool breeze playing with her hair. I was tempted to ask if I could help tuck that stray strand behind her ear, but then I remembered this was *not* a Bollywood movie. I played it safe and kept my hands to myself.

"So," she started, breaking the silence again, "What's the real story, Gaurav? I mean, you seem like a pretty chill guy. What's with the solo vibe?"

Ah, here it comes. The deeper questions. The ones that no amount of pre-date rehearsal can prepare you for. I took a deep breath and leaned back, staring at the water for a second.

"To be honest, I've been... I guess... focused on work, you know? Between coding and taking care of Hardy, I haven't really had time for, well, *this*." I gestured between us. "And, you know, relationships. They haven't exactly been my strong suit."

She looked at me with genuine curiosity, not judgment. "What happened with the last one? You said something earlier about a girl breaking your heart?"

Ah, the dreaded ex-conversation. My brain went into overdrive, trying to figure out how much to say without sounding like I was still hung up on it. But Prakriti had asked, and something told me being real with her was the way to go.

"Yeah," I nodded. "It was one of those 'we were just too different' situations. She wanted different things—bigger things. A whole different kind of life. And me? I was happy just... living simple, you know? With my work, Hardy, and, uh, black T-shirts."

Prakriti smiled softly. "So, she wanted more than you could give."

"Yeah, something like that. We both realized it wasn't going to work, and it was better to end it before things got worse. But, I guess after that, I kinda swore off dating for a while. Thought I'd focus on things I could control, like work. And well, here I am."

There was a pause, not awkward but thoughtful. Prakriti was clearly thinking, and I was bracing myself for her response.

"You know," she said slowly, "it's kind of refreshing hearing that. Most guys would just give a basic answer, like 'It didn't work out,' and move on. But you're being honest, and I respect that."

I felt my shoulders relax a little. "Well, honesty is the best policy, right?" I joked.

"Or the only policy when you're trying to impress someone," she added with a smirk.

"Touché." I laughed, feeling the tension in the air ease up again.

"So, how about you?" I asked, turning the tables. "Any exes in your rear-view mirror?"

Prakriti sighed, leaning back against the bench. "I had a relationship during college. We were good friends, and it kind of just... happened. But after a while, I realized we weren't right for each other. He didn't get my passion for writing. I mean, really get it. You know how some people nod and say, 'Yeah, that's cool,' but don't actually understand? It was like that."

I nodded. "Yeah, I get that. So you broke it off?"

"Yeah," she said, her voice soft. "It wasn't easy, but I had to. Writing is a huge part of who I am, and if someone doesn't get that... well, it's a deal-breaker."

There was a moment of understanding between us, and for once, I didn't feel the need to fill the silence. It was like we were both okay just being there, in that moment, sharing bits of our lives that we normally kept hidden.

And then, because the universe has a weird sense of timing, my phone buzzed. I glanced down and saw a message from *Hardy's Tank Alert*. Apparently, someone was trying to stage a jailbreak from the turtle tank at home.

I chuckled, showing Prakriti the alert. "Looks like Hardy's getting into trouble. I think he's plotting something."

She laughed. "Well, maybe he's jealous that you're out here having fun without him."

"Jealous Hardy is not something I want to deal with," I said, shaking my head. "That guy's already got trust issues."

Prakriti laughed again, and I could tell she was having fun. It wasn't some over-the-top movie date; it was simple, real, and honestly? That felt better than any over-planned, fancy outing.

We chatted some more—about random stuff, life, favorite books, and her love for writing. She even gave me a few recommendations that I *swore* I would check out. But the night was starting to wear on, and I could tell she was getting tired.

"So," she said as we reached the parking lot, "what now?"

I grinned, pulling out my invisible playbook. "Well, since I've nailed every step of this 'unofficial date,' I say we call it a success and head home. Don't want to push my luck."

She smiled, nodding. "Yeah, this was fun. Let's do it again sometime."

As we hopped on the bike, the night air felt different—lighter, maybe because I didn't screw up. And as we rode back, the silence between us wasn't the awkward kind. It was just... peaceful.

When I dropped her off near her home, she smiled at me, and for a second, I thought maybe I should say something cool, something memorable. But instead, I just said, "Take care, Prakriti."

"You too, Gaurav," she replied with that warm smile, the kind that could melt even Hardy's cold reptilian heart.

As I rode away, I couldn't help but feel like maybe this wasn't the last "unofficial date." Maybe it was just the beginning of something else.

Note from the writer*: Alright, folks. This was quite the ride, wasn't it? I bet you're wondering if I'm going to turn this into a slow-burn romance or if Hardy's jailbreak plan is going to take center stage. Honestly, even I don't know yet. But I do know this: sometimes, life throws out-of-syllabus questions at you, and you just have to wing it—whether it's on a date or figuring out what to wear when all you own is black.*

But don't worry, we're just getting started here. Stay tuned, because the adventure continues... and maybe Hardy's plotting something after all.

5

The Almost 'I Love You' Moment

A few weeks passed, and let me tell you, folks, this coding life wasn't getting any easier, but the little dopamine hits from Prakriti's texts? Totally worth it. Of course, Hardy was getting jealous by the minute, glaring at me from his tank like, *"Bro, where's my quality time?"*

Let me give you a pro tip here: if you ever want to avoid doing something productive, fall in love. I swear, my mind was less on Python and more on Prakriti every day. Seriously, between staring at the code and staring at her Instagram pictures, one of them was giving me *way* more bugs to fix. Spoiler: it wasn't the code.

Anyway, there I was, feeding Mr. Hardy (who was still plotting his tank break, by the way), when my phone pinged. Prakriti had posted another photo, and guess what? Yours truly was tagged in it again. This woman knows how to make a guy's day. I liked it, of course. Not too fast—didn't want to seem *too* eager, you know? Gotta play it cool. Like, "Oh hey, just casually checking my phone, no big deal."

You ever notice how much emotional labor goes into pretending to be chill? It's exhausting.

I wanted to text her a smooth, "Good morning, sunshine!" but then thought, *Too much? What if she thinks I'm one of those overly eager types?* And just like that, the most basic morning text became a 10-minute internal debate. I ended up not sending anything. Classic.

Later, I posted a pic of the two of us from our "unofficial date" on Instagram. Now, normally, I'm not one to post too much, but I figured, why not? It was a solid picture. We looked good together, and Hardy didn't need to know about this moment of social media PDA.

Prakriti liked the picture within minutes (and yes, I kept checking). Then came the comment: *"It was a really wonderful day."*

And boom! Just like that, I was grinning like an idiot in front of my turtle.

"Don't judge me, Hardy. It's called love," I muttered.

He blinked slowly. I swear, that turtle's side-eye game is stronger than any shade thrown by an ex.

Now, let's not kid ourselves here—life wasn't all romance montages and slow walks by the river. No sir, it was mostly me drowning in code and fighting deadlines. Prakriti and I texted regularly, sure, but the voice conversations? Yeah, those were rare. Something about hearing her voice made me all jittery, like a teenager waiting for their crush to pick up the phone in the days before texting.

And then there were the video calls. Ah yes, the famous "show me what Hardy's doing" calls. Listen, Hardy's become the unexpected MVP of this whole situation. Who knew that a turtle could be the ultimate wingman? Every time I showed her Hardy's antics, she'd laugh, and I'd secretly thank the universe for giving me this slow-moving reptile as an ally. You know you're deep into the love game when even your turtle's getting more screen time than you.

Days passed, then weeks, and between both our work schedules, we didn't get to meet up for another date. No more fancy cafes, no more riverside walks. Just text after text. I missed her, man. A lot. But hey, relationships in the adult world are like debugging a really stubborn program—you just have to keep working on it, even when it doesn't always make sense.

I found myself thinking about her during meetings, during lunch breaks, and pretty much any time I wasn't actively typing on the keyboard. Even Hardy, who I thought was a great listener (he really is), was starting to roll his eyes. Yeah, I said it—*turtle eye-rolls*. They're real.

And if you think this is all leading up to a grand romantic gesture, hold your horses. I'm a software developer, not a Bollywood hero. But hey, who knows what'll happen next? Maybe I'll plan the next big move, or maybe Hardy will make a jailbreak and go viral, winning Prakriti over once and for all.

Note from the writer:*Listen, friends, if you're thinking, "Is this guy really talking about a turtle this much?"—yes, yes, I am. And don't pretend Hardy's not the real star of this story. But hey, life's not all coding and awkward first dates. Sometimes, it's the quiet moments, the random texts, and even the help of a sneaky turtle that keep things interesting.So, stay tuned. Will there be another unofficial date? Will Hardy finally break out of his tank? Will Gaurav ever figure out what to wear besides black? You'll just have to keep reading.*

A few more days went by, and I was starting to feel like the main character in one of those slow-burn romance movies. You know, the kind where the guy spends half the movie doing awkward things, overanalyzing every conversation, while his turtle judges him from a distance? Yeah, that was me. I bet Hardy was narrating this entire saga to his little turtle friends, probably calling me "The Clueless One."

One evening, while I was knee-deep in code, another notification popped up on my screen. And no, it wasn't the usual bug report from work. It was Prakriti. The one text that made my otherwise boring day seem interesting.

"Hey, how's Hardy doing?"

She'd ask about Hardy. Of course, she would. At this point, I was convinced Hardy was the reason she still talked to me.

"He's doing good, just planning his next escape from the tank. You know how it is." I sent that off with a chuckle, imagining Hardy plotting his little turtle revolution.

She replied almost instantly, "Hahaha, poor thing. Maybe he needs more attention."

At that moment, I could practically hear Hardy laughing in the background. Attention? I was feeding this turtle, cleaning his tank, and using him as my secret weapon in this relationship. He was getting more attention than I was!

As I tried to think of something witty to say, my phone buzzed again. Another text from Prakriti: "By the way, wanna grab dinner tomorrow? If Hardy allows, of course"

Dinner? Another unofficial date? My heart did that thing again—you know, skipping beats like it was practicing for a marathon.

"Sure, I'll check with Hardy, but I'm free," I replied, because apparently, all life decisions now ran through my turtle.

She sent a laughing emoji, and that was that. I had another *not-a-date* lined up.

So the next day, after spending far too much time contemplating what to wear (hint: it was black), I got ready. Hardy gave me his usual disapproving look, which I interpreted as, *"Bro, you need some new clothes."* I ignored him because I didn't need that kind of negativity in my life right now.

I reached the restaurant a little early, as usual. I was sitting there, scrolling through Instagram, probably liking a few of her photos and overthinking the captions, when she walked in. And wow, she looked even better than last time. My heart didn't just skip beats—it did a full-on drum solo.

I stood up, all casual-like, trying not to look too eager, and waved. She smiled and walked over, and just like that, I was back in "don't mess this up" mode. You know the one, where every movement is calculated? How you hold your glass, how you sit, how you breathe, how you exist? Yeah, it was that all over again.

"Hey," she said as she sat down, looking at me like I was the most normal guy in the world and not someone internally panicking about saying the right thing.

"Hey," I replied, trying to sound as cool as a guy who spends 90% of his time with a turtle could.

We ordered dinner—nothing too fancy, but nothing too casual either. It's a fine line, people. And then, out of nowhere, she hit me with a question that I did *not* see coming.

"So, Gaurav, what's your biggest fear?"

Wait, what? I thought we were having pasta and talking about Hardy, not diving into existential philosophy!

Now, this could've gone one of two ways. I could've given her the real answer, something like, *"failure"* or *"heights"*—you know, the classic stuff. But this was Prakriti, and I wanted to impress her, make her laugh. So, I went for broke.

"Honestly? Hardy escaping the tank and leading a turtle uprising in my apartment," I said, keeping a completely straight face.

She blinked at me for a second, processing what I just said, and then burst out laughing. Success! Nailed it.

"That's your biggest fear? A turtle revolution?" she giggled, wiping away a tear from laughing.

"Hey, you joke now, but when they rise up and start demanding lettuce at all hours, you'll be sorry!" I continued, leaning into the joke.

"Okay, I'll keep that in mind," she said, still smiling. "But seriously, I think Hardy's safe. I'm more worried about you."

We both laughed, and for the first time in what felt like forever, I wasn't overthinking it. I was just enjoying the moment. The conversation flowed, with jokes about turtles, coding disasters, and her writing projects. I told her how Hardy had become my unofficial therapist, and she laughed again, making the night feel effortless.

As the dinner wrapped up, and we were walking out of the restaurant, I realized something. This wasn't just another "unofficial date" anymore. Something was there—something real. Maybe it was the fact that I could joke around with her, or maybe it was the way she smiled when she talked about her writing. Either way, it felt good. Natural.

We stood by my non-sponsored black Continental GT 650 again, and I handed her the helmet.

"Thanks for tonight, Gaurav," she said, putting it on. "And give Hardy my love. Tell him I'll help him with the revolution if he needs."

I smiled, revving up the engine. "Will do. But you know, after tonight, you might have to help me, too."

She laughed, hopped on the bike, and we rode off into the night.

As we cruised down the open road, the cold wind brushing past us, I couldn't help but feel like I was in some kind of slow-motion movie. You know, the kind where the guy looks super cool riding a bike, except I probably looked like I was trying not to shiver while also overthinking everything. We passed a few resorts, and then, out of nowhere, Prakriti said something.

My heart nearly jumped out of my chest. *Did she just say "I love you"?* My mind went into overdrive. Was this it? The moment? Was my entire life just about to change?

I panicked, I'm not gonna lie. I didn't hear it properly, but my brain immediately latched onto the words *"I love you."* I could already see Hardy giving me a high-five later, saying, *"I told you she liked me!"*

But, just to be sure, I leaned in a little and asked, "Sorry, what did you say?"

She pointed to a sign on the side of the road, completely unaware of the emotional rollercoaster she'd just put me through. "La Vue Resort," she said with a smile.

Oh. Right. Of course. She was pointing out the name of a resort, not declaring her undying love for me. Classic Gaurav, overthinking everything once again. I felt my face heat up, not from the cold wind but from sheer embarrassment.

I let out a breath I didn't even know I was holding and tried to play it cool. "Yeah, La Vue Resort, looks nice!" I nodded, as if I hadn't just experienced an entire imaginary love confession in the last five seconds.

The cold breeze continued to flow around us as we rode on, the stars twinkling above. It was peaceful. There was no need to talk, no rush, just the two of us cruising through the night. I wanted to freeze this moment. Well, not *that* moment of confusion about the "I love you," but the calmness, the simplicity of it all. I didn't need anything more—just us, the road, and maybe, somewhere in the back of my mind, a small hope that one day, the "I love you" might actually happen. For real this time.

Note from the writer:*Alright, so I know what you're thinking: "Did Gaurav really think she said 'I love you' after, what, two semi-dates and a lot of turtle talk?" Well, yes. Welcome to the inner workings of an overactive mind in love, where every word, every look, every pause is dissected like a science experiment.And hey, we've all been there—thinking someone said something they totally didn't. Maybe it's a sign I need to focus more on what's actually happening and not on the future episodes of "Gaurav and Prakriti's love saga." But in my defense, I blame the romantic vibe of the night. And also Hardy. Always Hardy.*

6

The Silence Between Us

As the months passed by, I still couldn't shake the epic misunderstanding at La View Resort. For those few seconds, I thought, "This is it. The moment!" Turns out, it wasn't love she was pointing at—just a fancy signboard. Life, you know, it really loves to mess with your head sometimes. But hey, I'll admit it, the false hope gave me a few sleepless nights.

Life wasn't done playing with me just yet. I got promoted at work, which should have been a high. But like life enjoys pulling the rug from under you, this promotion came with a catch. I had to move to Guwahati. The thought of being away from Prakriti felt like a sucker punch straight to the gut. One minute I'm imagining a future here, the next minute, I'm packing boxes to leave. Yeah, it's one of those "life is complicated" moments. The promotion was great for my career, sure, but it felt like a death sentence for whatever was budding between me and Prakriti.

"I have to report to the Guwahati head office soon. I'll miss you," I texted her, trying to keep it cool while my insides churned.

"So, when are you coming back?" she replied.

"Actually... I'm shifting there for good," I typed, staring at my screen for a second, feeling the weight of those words. I hit send, hoping she wouldn't hate me.

Her reply came quickly, and when I saw it, my heart shattered: "I'll miss you too."

You know that feeling when someone says the exact thing you were dreading to hear? Yeah, this was that. Like a quiet "game over" screen flashing in my mind. My head screamed, "Do something, idiot!" before my fingers started typing.

"Can we meet before I leave?" I sent in desperation, holding on to the hope that this wouldn't be the last time we'd sit together.

"I was thinking the same," she replied, and it almost felt like a sliver of light breaking through the fog of what was starting to feel like a goodbye.

When we finally met, it was tough. The kind of tough where you don't know whether to smile or cry. I could see the sadness in her eyes—hidden behind that same sweet smile I'd grown so used to. Cute as always, but today, that smile hurt.

We rode in silence. No small talk, no jokes, just the quiet hum of my bike and the cold wind cutting through us as we cruised over Koliabhomora Bridge. This bridge, man—it had seen us through so many moments. I always found small ways to surprise her here. Today was no different. I reached into my jacket, pulling out a pink rose and a letter I had written, crafting her face with the letters of her name. I handed it to her, my heart in my throat.

She blushed, her cheeks turning that soft red that made her look even more beautiful. She leaned closer to me, but something held her back from wrapping her arms around me. Maybe it was uncertainty, maybe it was something else.

Who knows?

"I'll miss all these moments with you," she whispered, her voice barely cutting through the wind.

"I will too," I managed, and just like that, we fell into silence again.

We didn't stop. We kept riding, all the way towards Kaziranga. No destination, no plan, just two people trying to stretch time as far as it would go.

"I might come to Guwahati, though," she said, breaking the silence. "I've applied for a PhD at Gauhati University."

And just like that, hope flickered inside me.

"I really hope you crack the interview," I said, feeling lighter.

"I'll try my best, Gaurav."

Right then, I realized something. Maybe this isn't goodbye. Maybe this is just another twist in our story. And maybe, just maybe, this is the part where the universe decides to be a little kinder.

Note from the writer: *If you're still hoping for that grand confession of love, well, join the club. I'm over here breaking the fourth wall with you, screaming at these two to just admit their feelings already! But no, life isn't that simple. Or maybe they're just really good at prolonging the inevitable. Let's see where this roller-coaster takes us.*

The air grew heavier as we neared the edge of Kaziranga. The sun had started its slow descent, painting the sky in soft pinks and oranges. It was that kind of evening that you want to bottle up, keeping it safe for the hard days when everything feels out of control. We stopped by the roadside, not because we had to, but because the ride couldn't last forever.

I switched off the engine, the silence between us amplifying the sounds of nature around us. Birds were heading home, crickets already starting their evening concert. Prakriti stood beside me, leaning against the railing that overlooked the vast greenery stretching into the horizon. For a moment, it felt like the world had paused.

"I don't want this to be our last ride," she said softly, still staring at the sunset.

My heart clenched. I didn't want this to be the last either, but what could I say? Life was pulling us in different directions, and I didn't have the power to rewrite that script.

"We've had a lot of good rides," I said, trying to keep things light, though my voice betrayed me. "And who knows, maybe we'll have more. You might crack that PhD, and then we'll be riding through Guwahati, dodging traffic instead of cows."

She smiled, a soft laugh escaping her lips. "Yeah, maybe."

I reached out, my hand brushing against hers. For a second, I considered pulling her into a hug, holding her close and telling her everything I was too scared to say. But the moment passed, and I let my hand drop back to my side. Some things were better left unsaid for now.

The sun dipped lower, and reality began to seep back in. It was time to go. Time to leave behind this chapter of our lives and start the next. I start the bike to life once more, and she hopped on behind me, her hands finally resting gently on my back.

As we rode back, the wind felt different—colder, more final. Neither of us spoke, the silence between us heavy with unspoken words. But maybe that was okay. Maybe some things didn't need to be said right away. Maybe this wasn't the end, just a pause, like a book waiting for its next chapter.

When I dropped her off, I saw the sadness in her eyes again. She turned to go but paused, looking back at me one last time. "Take care, Gaurav."

"You too, Prakriti," I said, giving her a small smile. "This isn't goodbye."

She smiled back, though it was tinged with the same uncertainty we both felt. With one last wave, she disappeared into the evening light.

As I rode away, the familiar sounds of the city filling the air, I couldn't shake the feeling that this wasn't where our story ended. There was more, there had to be more. Life had its twists, sure, but sometimes, it gave you a second chance when you least expected it.

Note from the writer*: And that, dear readers, is where we leave Gaurav and Prakriti for now. Will fate bring them back together in Guwahati?Stick around for the next chapter, because trust me, this ride is far from over.*

7

The Turtle Whisperer and Late-Night Love Calls

I'm in Guwahati now, but I can't shake the feeling that I've left something behind. Or rather, someone—Prakriti. It's strange, isn't it? Back in Tezpur, we didn't meet every day, but knowing she was close by made things feel... easier, lighter. Now, even though we talk all the time, I feel the weight of distance more than I ever expected.

It took me about a week to settle down here, setting up my life in this new city, and Prakriti and I have been keeping in touch constantly. Her voice on the phone is like a melody I never want to stop hearing. And here's the funny thing—our late-night calls have gotten longer and longer. I mean, if there's any silver lining to this move, it's that we've become even closer in a way I hadn't anticipated. I guess distance really does make the heart grow fonder... or it just makes us stay up later, exhausted but unwilling to say goodnight.

Oh, and don't worry—Hardy's here too. Of course, I couldn't leave the boss behind! He's made himself at home, but the first couple of days were rough. Poor guy wasn't eating for two whole days, probably as confused and unsettled by the move as I was. And Prakriti, being the kind soul she is, actually got so worried about him that she stopped eating too. Can you imagine that? She was more upset about Hardy than I was! I don't know what's worse—the fact that my turtle has that kind of influence over her, or that I'm slightly jealous he gets more attention from her than I do.

But things are back to normal now. Hardy's back to his old self, strutting around the place like he owns it, and Prakriti's eating again, thank God. As for me? I've settled into the new routine, into this new life. I'm stable now. But... I miss her. I miss her in a way that's hard to explain.

You know, it's funny. You'd think technology would make it easier, with the endless texting and calling. But the truth is, no number of late-night phone calls can replace the feeling of just being next to her. Of seeing her smile up close, hearing her laugh in real time, without the lag of a network connection. Sometimes, I wish I could just walk up to her like I used to, or surprise her with some random chocolates on a whim.

But here I am, in Guwahati, and she's there. Life is what it is, right? If only Hardy could offer some wise turtle advice, but alas—he's just here for the lettuce.

Note from the writer: *Yes, we've entered the "I miss you" phase of the long-distance situation. Things are looking a little bleak for our guy Gaurav, but hey, we're rooting for him.*

Life in Guwahati was... well, let's just say it wasn't as glamorous as I imagined. You know how in the movies, when the protagonist moves to a new city, everything is exciting, and they get their life together in a montage set to upbeat music? Yeah, well, my life in Guwahati is less "cool montage" and more "accidentally spilling coffee on myself at 7 a.m. while trying to figure out why my Wi-Fi keeps disconnecting."

At least I have Hardy here to keep me company. Except, let's be real—Hardy's not the emotional support pet you'd think. He's more like a silent roommate who just watches me go about my sad little routine. If he could talk, I'm pretty sure he'd tell me to get a grip and stop staring at my phone like it's going to magically teleport Prakriti to my doorstep. But since he can't talk, I'm just left to interpret his disapproving side-eye while I scroll through old pictures of us.

Speaking of Prakriti, we've been talking constantly. You know, the late-night, deep conversations that make you feel like you're starring in your own little romance movie—except, of course, without the actual romance happening in person. Our calls stretch into the night, and at this point, I'm pretty sure my sleep cycle is as broken as my heart. (Okay, okay, I'm being dramatic. But come on, I miss her!)

The other day, she asked about Hardy again. You'd think she was more emotionally invested in his well-being than mine. "Is Hardy eating okay now?" she asked, with genuine concern. And there I was, like, "Yeah, Hardy's fine. Me, on the other hand? I'm barely surviving on instant noodles and existential dread, but don't worry, the turtle's thriving."

Of course, she was worried when Hardy wasn't eating for two days after the move. And when I told her, she actually stopped eating too. I swear, Hardy's got some sort of strange power over her. Like, I might be the one with feelings for her, but Hardy's the one she truly cares about. I half-expect him to start stealing the spotlight in our relationship.

"Hardy's back to his old self," I told her, feeling like I was giving her the best news of the century. "He's munching on lettuce like nothing ever happened." I'm pretty sure I could have told her I won the lottery, and she'd have been less excited than hearing about Hardy's renewed appetite.

We've been texting a lot more too. Sometimes, the conversations are deep and meaningful. Other times, they're just... well, let's say we end up sending random memes at 2 a.m., both of us too tired to function but neither wanting to say goodnight. And yes, I still haven't figured out how to casually text "I miss you" without sounding clingy. So, naturally, I just resort to "Hey, how's Hardy doing?" as if that's going to get me the same emotional connection.

But you know what? In a weird way, it feels like we're getting closer, even though we're miles apart. Our conversations are longer, our connection feels deeper, and, well, I'm learning a lot about what I can talk about for hours on end. Apparently, turtles are a much better conversation topic than I thought.

Still, I can't help but feel like something's missing. Guwahati's nice and all, but without Prakriti here, it feels... incomplete. Like, the city has all the noise, the hustle, and the chaos, but none of the calm that she brings into my life.

And don't even get me started on the nights. You know how in romance novels, the hero stands by the window, staring dramatically into the distance, pining for his love? Yeah, that's not me. I'm usually just sprawled out on my couch, mindlessly binge-watching Netflix, wondering why the algorithm keeps recommending rom-coms when I'm clearly trying to avoid all things romantic. Thanks, Netflix, for rubbing salt in the wound.

But at least I have Hardy. Or at least, that's what I keep telling myself. He's lounging in his tank, oblivious to my existential crisis. If only he could offer me some wise, turtle-like advice. Something like, "Dude, just tell her how you feel" or "Stop being such a wimp and go visit her." But nope—he's just chilling, chewing on lettuce, and living his best life.

Note from the writer: *If you've made it this far, congrats! You're now fully invested in the romantic saga of Gaurav, Prakriti, and their surprisingly influential turtle, Hardy. Don't worry, we're getting to the part where things get interesting... or maybe they don't. Stay tuned, folks. Hardy might take over the story at this rate.*

8

Surprise! And Other Unplanned Moments

After three months in Guwahati, I decided it was time to give Prakriti a surprise visit. The plan? Classic: a bunch of small gifts, some flowers, chocolates (her second love after momos), and a pair of earrings because, why not? I have no clue about earrings, but hey, it's the thought that counts, right? Oh, and letters—three of them. I had way too much to say, and since I couldn't spill it all at once without sounding like a maniac, I figured handwritten letters would be perfect. Physical letters have that emotional attachment. Or at least, that's what rom-coms have taught me.

Now, I know you're all worried about Hardy. Don't panic—he's fine. He's got an automatic feeder because, yes, my turtle lives like a king. His basking lights are all set to sunrise and sunset mode, so he's basically living in a spa. Honestly, he's probably having a better time than I am on this road trip.

So, I decided to hit the road late Friday night. My stealth mode was on—I even called Prakriti, pretending to still be in Guwahati so she wouldn't suspect a thing. This surprise had to be epic.

I started my bat-mobile (which, in case you forgot, is black because apparently, I have a theme) and rolled out around 10:30 PM. The highway was quiet, with the occasional truck zooming past. My excitement was at an all-time high—I just wanted to skip this whole riding part and get to the good stuff, you know, like being face-to-face with Prakriti instead of pretending to care about highway speed limits.

Everything was going smoothly... until it wasn't.

All of a sudden, my rear wheel decided it wanted to reenact a scene from *Fast & Furious*. It drifted to the right, and I was going at about 80-90 kmph. My heart skipped more beats than a DJ at a club. Instinct kicked in—I let go of the accelerator and avoided the brakes, just letting the bike stabilize on its own. If you're wondering how I didn't crash, well, let's just say I was 80% skill and 20% pure luck. (Okay, maybe it was the other way around, but we'll keep that between us.)

Turns out, a tanker had flipped over about 300 meters ahead, and diesel had leaked all over the road. Yep, slippery as an ice rink. So, near-death experience aside, I made it through unscathed. No scratches, no bruises—just me, my bike, and a sudden appreciation for life.

I finally reached Tezpur at around 2:45 AM. And now, there I was—sitting in the quiet night, staring at the horizon, waiting for the sunrise like some sort of nocturnal stalker. I didn't sleep. How could I? I was way too excited. I just wanted to hit fast-forward and skip to the part where I see Prakriti's face light up when I surprise her.

Of course, Hardy was probably asleep back home, oblivious to my heroic journey, munching away thanks to his luxury feeder. That little guy doesn't know how lucky he has it.

But here I was, a human, waiting for the sun to rise. Typical, right?

As I sat there, staring at the horizon like some kind of overly dramatic movie protagonist, I realized something: time does **not** move faster just because you want it to. Seriously, where's a good time machine when you need one? I had already checked my phone a thousand times, not for the time, mind you, but for any sign of Prakriti waking up and ruining the surprise by messaging me with her usual "Good morning, what are you up to?"

I kept refreshing the clock like I was waiting for a software update. Spoiler alert: still no sunrise.

At some point, I began to question my life choices. Like, *Why didn't I leave earlier?* Or better yet, *Why didn't I just take a train?* But then again, arriving on a train doesn't exactly scream "surprise hero" as much as rolling up on my bike like I'm auditioning for a low-budget action movie. And speaking of movies, I started having this really deep thought (blame the sleep deprivation): *Why isn't there a superhero who's just super good at waiting?* I mean, I'd probably crush that role.

Hardy, by the way, was probably living it up back in Guwahati—probably basking under his heat lamp, looking at his automatic feeder like, *Yeah, life's good.*

But back to me: I'm sitting in Tezpur, bike parked, with my bag full of gifts like some kind of nocturnal Santa Claus, and no amount of squinting at the sky could make the sun rise faster. I even considered doing push-ups to kill time but then thought, *No, what if I'm all sweaty when I see Prakriti?* No one wants their surprise visit to be remembered as "the time you smelled like a gym locker."

Finally, FINALLY, the sky started to lighten. It was that magical moment when the first rays of sun poke through the darkness... and I suddenly realized how **tired** I was. Seriously, who knew waiting could be so exhausting?

As soon as the sun was high enough to seem reasonable (aka 7:00 AM), I texted Prakriti, pretending I had just woken up in Guwahati. Oh yeah, stealth mode still engaged.

"Good morning! What's your plan today?"

Now, here's the thing: if she had said something like "I'm just staying in," I'd have had to figure out a whole new plan. But no, like the universe was giving me a high five, she replied:

"I'm going to the market today. Just some errands. What about you?"

Perfect. The stars had aligned. I was about to crash her day in the best way possible.

I started the bike and began to roll out, my mind racing faster than my bike. Now, don't get me wrong, I had the whole surprise visit fantasy playing out in my head: I'd find her in the market, she'd see me, her jaw would drop, and we'd run to each other in slow motion like some sappy Bollywood scene. But in real life? I was just hoping I didn't trip over something and end up embarrassing myself. Or worse, awkwardly waving at the wrong person.

And so, off I went, trying not to think about how absurdly early it still was for a surprise visit. I mean, if I were her, I'd be wondering why some random guy was showing up at 7 AM with flowers and earrings. *But hey, romance is 10% planning and 90% being mildly irrational,* right?

As I cruised toward the market, I could feel the excitement building. Prakriti was about to get the surprise of her life, and I was about to finally see her after three long months. The only thing I had to worry about now was my heart racing faster than my bike.

Well, that, and not dying on the highway again.

As I rode toward the market, the excitement kept building—along with the cold reality that I still had no clue what I'd actually *say* to Prakriti. Sure, I had the whole "surprise visit" angle down, but beyond that? Nothing. What if I just stood there like an awkward statue, holding flowers, chocolates, and a fancy pair of earrings, and all she did was stare at me like, "Uh, thanks?"

The overthinking began.

"What if she doesn't like the earrings?"
"What if I picked the wrong chocolates?"
"What if I totally butcher the moment and end up stammering like an idiot?"

At this point, my internal monologue was more dramatic than any soap opera. And trust me, Hardy would've been laughing if turtles had any sense of humor. I could almost hear him saying, *"Bro, this is why you're not a superhero—too much anxiety for surprise missions."*

But I couldn't back out now. I had come too far, physically and emotionally, to let the fear of a potential awkward conversation stop me. Plus, I'd already committed to wearing this surprise-visit grin that was now permanently stuck to my face like I'd just won the lottery.

And then, I saw her.

I had just turned the corner into the market, and there she was, casually browsing through some fruit stands like she wasn't about to have her entire morning flipped upside down. It's funny how in those moments, time seems to slow down, but also, your mind goes completely blank. I had written her **three letters** full of feelings, thoughts, and all the things I couldn't say in person, but right now? My brain was like, *"Say hi. Just say hi."*

I parked my bike a little away, so she wouldn't spot me too soon, then grabbed my bag of gifts like I was on a secret mission. (Spoiler alert: I wasn't very stealthy. Apparently, trying to sneak through a crowded market with a big smile on your face and a bag full of random romantic stuff isn't exactly subtle.)

And then, in the most cinematic way possible—okay, not really, more like the real-world awkward way—I walked right up behind her.

"Hey, stranger."

She turned around, and the look on her face was priceless. At first, there was confusion—like, *Wait, did I just imagine Gaurav's voice?* And then, as it all clicked, her eyes widened, and she blinked a few times as if she were seeing a ghost.

"Oh my God! What are you doing here?!" she gasped, her face lighting up with that smile that made the entire exhausting journey worth it.

"Surprise!" I said, trying to keep it cool like I hadn't been freaking out about this moment for the past three hours. "I thought I'd drop by for a visit."

She laughed, clearly taken aback. "You didn't tell me you were coming! I would've—"

"That's the point of a surprise," I interrupted with a grin, finally feeling like I nailed my first line.

I handed her the flowers, and she blushed, just like she did that first time on our unofficial date. "These are for you. And... I got you these too." I reached into my bag and pulled out the chocolates and the earrings, hoping she wouldn't think I'd gone completely overboard.

Her eyes went wide again. "You really didn't have to... I mean, this is—wow!"

Now, I know what you're thinking. This is the part where everything falls into place, where we have the perfect romantic moment, and everything I planned works out beautifully, right? Well, almost.

I held out the letters, feeling like some kind of 19th-century poet who was too shy to speak his heart. "And I, uh... wrote you these. Because I didn't think I could say everything I wanted to say out loud."

Prakriti looked at the letters, then at me, clearly touched—but before she could say anything, one of the market vendors loudly dropped a box of apples nearby, completely shattering the moment.

Cue me trying not to laugh at the timing. *Because of course*, right? Fourth-wall break alert: this is exactly the kind of thing that only happens in real life. In movies, the world pauses when two people share a moment like this. In my world? Random fruit-related interruptions.

We both burst out laughing, and for a second, it felt like all the nervousness and uncertainty melted away. She took the letters from me, still smiling. "I don't even know what to say. You showing up here like this... this is probably the sweetest thing anyone's ever done."

I shrugged, trying to play it cool. "Well, I figured you were missing me. And Hardy, of course."

"Of course," she echoed, still grinning. "How is he?"

"Living the dream," I said. "Boss of the house, as always."

She laughed again, and just like that, we fell back into the rhythm we always had, as if no time had passed. Sure, I had nearly wiped out on a diesel-slick road to get here, and sure, I had spent half the night stressing about everything that could go wrong—but none of that mattered now.

We decided to grab some breakfast at a nearby café, and as we walked there, it hit me: no matter how much I overthink or how many times I try to plan out every little detail, real life is always going to throw in its share of unexpected moments.

As we made our way to the café, I couldn't help but smile at how easily things had fallen back into place. Prakriti chatted about her morning, her laughter filling the air like music. It felt so natural, like no time had passed since I'd last seen her.

Once we settled into a small corner table, I couldn't resist teasing her about the market incident. "So, how do you feel about spontaneous apple showers?" I asked, grinning.

She rolled her eyes playfully. "Next time, I'll bring an umbrella just in case. But seriously, this is the best surprise. I can't believe you drove all this way!"

"Anything for you," I said, trying to keep it light, though inside, I was beaming. "Plus, I couldn't let you hog all the momos and chocolates, could I?"

As we placed our orders—two steaming cups of coffee and a heaping plate of their famous pancakes—she took a moment to glance over the letters I had given her, their edges neatly folded. "Can I read these now?" she asked, her curiosity piqued.

"Of course! But maybe save the deep emotional stuff for after breakfast? I'd rather not tear up into my pancakes," I joked.

"Fair enough," she chuckled, but I could tell she was eager. The anticipation in her eyes reminded me of a kid on Christmas morning, and it made my heart swell.

"Alright, I think I'll read one of these now," she declared, picking up the first letter.

I watched her carefully as she unfolded it, my heart racing in rhythm with her soft gasps and smiles as she read.

With each line, I could see her expression shifting—first to surprise, then to something deeper.

"Gaurav," she said softly, looking up after finishing the first letter. "You really put a lot into these. They're… beautiful." Her voice was filled with sincerity, and I felt a warmth spread through me.

"Thanks! I just wanted to express what I couldn't say on the phone or in person," I replied, trying to downplay the sudden wave of vulnerability. "You know how I get when I try to talk about my feelings."

She nodded, her eyes sparkling. "Yeah, it's like watching a deer caught in headlights."

I laughed, but there was a softness to the moment that wrapped around us like a warm blanket. "Exactly! So, letters it was."

Prakriti took a deep breath, her fingers tracing the edges of the letter as she contemplated something. "I love that you took the time to write these, Gaurav. It means a lot to me."

"Honestly, it was a lot easier than trying to plan an epic speech," I admitted, feeling slightly sheepish. "And besides, I figured if it was on paper, it would be less likely to end up as a jumbled mess."

We shared a comfortable silence, punctuated by the occasional clink of cutlery and soft laughter from other patrons. It felt surreal being here, like stepping back into a well-worn groove that I hadn't realized I missed so much.

After a few minutes, she reached for the second letter. "Okay, I'm going for another one. You really need to stop writing so well; it's making me feel all the feels."

I smirked. "Well, I do what I can. A budding poet in the making."

As she read through the second letter, I couldn't help but steal glances at her, feeling an overwhelming sense of gratitude for this moment. The way her lips curved into a smile, the gentle way she bit her lip as she read—it was all a part of this perfect snapshot in time.

When she finished the second letter, she put it down and looked at me, her expression a mix of affection and seriousness. "Gaurav, you know that I've been thinking a lot about us lately."

I raised an eyebrow, a little nervous but eager to hear what she had to say. "Oh? Good thoughts, I hope?"

"Definitely good!" she reassured, her tone softening. "I just... I feel like we've both grown a lot in the past few months, and I love that we can still come back to each other like this."

"Yeah, it's like we've got our own little time capsule. No matter how far apart we are, we can always pick up right where we left off," I said, feeling a surge of hope.

"And that's something really special," she added, her eyes locking onto mine.

Just then, the waiter arrived with our order—fluffy pancakes stacked high, topped with a mountain of whipped cream and fresh fruits. The smell wafted toward us, interrupting the serious moment and bringing us back to the present.

"Breakfast is served!" the waiter declared with a smile, and I couldn't help but chuckle at how perfectly timed it was.

"Best distraction ever," Prakriti said, grinning. "We'll save the deep talks for later, but I want to finish these letters first."

"Deal!" I agreed, and we dove into the pancakes, the sweetness of the food mirroring the warmth in my chest.

As we indulged in breakfast, the conversation flowed effortlessly. We talked about everything—her plans for the day, my chaotic ride to Tezpur, and how Hardy was probably having a blast back at home.

At one point, as she recounted her last adventure in the market, I couldn't help but think about how this moment, this simple breakfast, was what I had been missing all along. No grand gestures, no elaborate plans—just two people who cared deeply for each other, sharing laughter, food, and the comfort of companionship.

When she finally finished reading all the letters, she looked at me, eyes bright. "Okay, now it's my turn to give you something."

"Oh? Is it a letter about how amazing I am?" I teased, winking.

She rolled her eyes playfully. "Not exactly. But I did get something for you, too."

She reached into her bag and pulled out a small box. I stared at it, slightly confused. "What's this?"

"Open it and find out," she encouraged, her excitement infectious.

I carefully opened the box to reveal a sleek keychain in the shape of a turtle. My heart melted a little at the gesture. "Is this...?"

"Yup! It's Hardy-inspired! I figured you could carry a piece of him with you whenever you're away," she explained, her cheeks flushing slightly.

"Prakriti, this is awesome! I love it!" I said, genuinely touched. "You're going to make him jealous if he finds out."

"Well, I have to keep him on his toes," she laughed, her eyes sparkling with mischief.

After breakfast, we decided to take a stroll through the market, the day unfolding with unexpected warmth and laughter. Each step felt lighter, filled with the promise of the moments to come. I knew that this surprise visit was just the beginning of a new chapter for us—one filled with shared adventures, spontaneous laughter, and a whole lot of love.

As we walked side by side, I felt a sense of contentment wash over me. Whatever challenges lay ahead, I was ready to face them head-on, as long as I had Prakriti by my side. And maybe even a little turtle wisdom from Hardy to guide me along the way.

Note from the Writer:Hey, you fabulous reader!

So, you've made it to Chapter 8—congrats! Just a quick note from your humble author here. If you think Gaurav's surprise visit is a whirlwind of excitement, just wait until you try planning your own surprise! Spoiler alert: it involves a lot of overthinking, awkward moments, and maybe a near-death experience or two (just kidding... kind of).

Remember, life is like a romantic comedy—full of unexpected twists, a dash of chaos, and a lead character who sometimes forgets that waiting for the sunrise is not a superhero skill. If you're laughing, you're doing it right! So, grab some popcorn (or momos, if you're feeling adventurous) and buckle up for more antics.

And don't worry; I promise the story won't suddenly take a turn into a serious documentary about the plight of turtles. At least, not yet.

Happy reading!

9
Whispers of the Heart

Those three days with Prakriti were *chef's kiss*—pure magic. I mean, if there was an award for "Most Blissful Days Spent in a Bubble of Love," I'd be a shoo-in. And yet, here I am, sitting in Guwahati, replaying every moment in my head like a sappy rom-com montage. It's funny how every time I'm with her, I find myself wanting to freeze time, just so I can bask in her presence a little longer. Her sweet voice? Like music. My endless stream of silly jokes? Somehow, she laughs. **Actual laughter, people.** Her smile—well, let's just say it makes my heart do this weird, happy dance that would probably make even Mr. Hardy cringe.

But here's the thing: I'm scared. Terrified, actually. What if she doesn't feel the same way? What if I'm just this guy throwing heart eyes all over the place, while she's thinking, *"Oh Gaurav, you're like... a really good friend!"* That fear? Yeah, it's like a bucket of cold water on my romantic daydreams.

Those three days were memorable—no, scratch that, they were legendary. Every second with Prakriti is etched in my brain like it's trying to compete with Hardy's slow-motion swimming sessions. But on that last day... oh boy, leaving her and heading back to Guwahati was brutal. I could see it in her eyes when she said, "I'm going to miss you, Gaurav. Don't leave me." Wait, actually, she didn't *say* it. She said it with her eyes—you know, that look. I *really* wanted to hear it from her lips, though. We were driving back. It was that perfect evening light, with forests stretching on either side of the road. You know, that kind of cinematic moment where if this were a movie, some soulful music would start playing? I couldn't miss it. "Prakriti," I said, trying to sound all calm, but inside, my heart was doing a drum solo. She looked at me, leaning in closer. "Hmmm?" she replied, her voice soft like a melody.

"I'm going to miss you," I said, holding my breath like I had just dropped the world's most profound statement. She just gently placed her hand on my arm, and in that moment, I felt the universe slow down. I was so nervous to hold her hand, but I did it anyway. And there it was—her soft, warm hand in mine. My heart was racing like I'd just chugged five cups of coffee, and everything around us blurred out. The moment was perfect. I wanted to say so many things, spill my heart out to her, but the fear of ruining it held me back. I just held her hand tighter, wondering if she felt what I did.

"I... I'll miss you, Prakriti," I stammered out again. What I wanted to say was something far bigger, something that would've changed everything between us. But of course, courage wasn't on my side that day.

"I'll miss you too, Gaurav," she said, and her voice—it lit me up from the inside out. Forget caffeine, that sentence was the real pick-me-up I needed. "Next week, I'll be in Guwahati for my PhD interview," she added after a pause.

"I'll be waiting for you," I said, still holding her hand. And when I squeezed it slightly tighter, I hoped she could feel all the unspoken words in that simple gesture.

Fast forward to now, and here I am in Guwahati, missing her like crazy. Mr. Hardy? He's fine, in case you're wondering. He's been chilling in his tank, looking at me like he's the king of the world—completely oblivious that I left him for three days. Maybe that automatic feeder spoiled him more than it should have. When I came back, he splashed around like, *"Oh, you're back? Cool, now feed me."* At least someone doesn't mind being left behind...

But as for me, every splash of water from Hardy feels like a tiny reminder of the moments I had with Prakriti. And, well, here we are—you and me—going through my romantic dilemmas together. I hope you're rooting for me, because if this doesn't work out, it's going to be a *long* conversation with Hardy about life, love, and heartbreak. But hey, at least I'll have a good listener, right?

As I sat in my room in Guwahati, staring at the ceiling, my thoughts were a messy jumble of Prakriti, her soft voice, and... Hardy. Yep, Hardy, my turtle, who seemed to care more about the automatic feeder than the emotional catastrophe I was going through. "You know, Hardy," I said aloud, glancing over at the little splash of water he made in the tank, "I don't get how you can live so peacefully. I'm over here overthinking every little moment, and you're just... swimming." He blinked at me. No help at all.

I sighed and lay back on the bed. **"Oh, hey, didn't notice you there,"** I say, breaking the fourth wall and looking right at you. **"Yeah, I'm in deep now. You know how it is—guy falls for girl, guy overthinks everything, guy's pet turtle doesn't even care. Classic."**

The moment replayed in my head, that drive back through the forest. The way the trees blurred by, the quiet hum of the bike, Prakriti's hand gently touching mine. My heart was beating like a drum solo in a rock band. **"I know** what you're thinking—'why didn't you just say something, Gaurav? Confess your feelings, dude!' Believe me, I had a whole speech planned, but then my brain decided to remind me that I'm a professional at overthinking."

I remembered the look in her eyes, like she was telling me not to leave. But of course, she didn't actually say it. And did I push for it? Nope. I just mumbled something lame like, "I'll miss you." Genius, right?

Now here I am, sitting in Guwahati, replaying that moment over and over. **"If this were a movie, she'd have said something dramatic like, 'Don't leave me,' and I'd have stayed. But no, life isn't a rom-com, and I chickened out. So here I am, holding her hand, saying nothing important, and hoping she'll read my mind."**

Fast-forward to now, and I'm still waiting for her message, overanalyzing everything. **"And Hardy? Well, he's still splashing water like he hasn't a care in the world. Honestly, sometimes I think he's the real star of my life."**

Hardy gave me another lazy splash, and I laughed. "Yeah, you're right, buddy. I'm over here drowning in my own thoughts, and you're just living the dream."

"But hey," I say to you, **"don't give up on me yet. There's still hope. Maybe next time, I'll actually get the courage to tell her how I really feel. Or, you know, I'll just continue to be a world-class overthinker. Stay tuned."**

And with that, I laid back, grinning to myself, as Hardy continued his nonchalant swim across the tank, completely unaware of the romantic drama unfolding just outside his glass walls.

Note from the Writer:*Ah, love. It makes you say things like, "I'll miss you" when you really want to say, "I never want to leave your side." But hey, baby steps, right? Maybe if Gaurav* *wasn't so busy overthinking every glance and touch, we'd have a confession by now. Meanwhile, Hardy the turtle remains the true emotional rock of this story—cool, calm, and probably wondering why his human keeps talking to himself.*

10
Baked Beans and Dreams

"I am coming to Guwahati! See you soon," a text flashed on my screen from Prakriti. It felt like I was floating on a cloud, maybe even the one where people say you can find your dreams—except I was just dreaming about her. "See you soon! I'm waiting," I replied, trying to sound cool but probably failing miserably.

Today was the day—the day she was interviewing for her PhD program. You'd think I was the one being interviewed with how nervous I felt! I swear, waiting for her was like watching paint dry—except I was more anxious and less colorful. So, naturally, I decided to arrive at the bus stand earlier than a caffeine addict at a coffee shop, wearing my best "supportive boyfriend" face.

Finally, she arrived. She looked absolutely stunning, strutting in with her laptop like a boss. Seriously, if confidence had a face, it would be hers. I wanted to lift her in my arms and declare my love to the world. But you know me—I'm not exactly the type to start an impromptu love festival. Instead, I settled for a hug that felt like a scene straight out of a rom-com.

We headed to a café near Gauhati University because, let's be real, nothing calms pre-interview jitters like English breakfast and tea. I knew she hadn't eaten anything, so I ordered the works. She was so engrossed in her research proposal, flipping through her file and peering at her laptop, that she forgot her stomach existed.

I couldn't let her starve while she was saving the academic world! So, I took a spoonful of baked beans and said, "I know you will do it, Prakriti," offering it to her like a love-struck waiter. She blushed and, after a moment of surprise, opened her mouth. I continued to feed her like a concerned mother bird, and I couldn't help but chuckle at my ridiculousness. Who knew romance would come with a side of baked beans?

"I think we should get going," she finally said after polishing off her tea.

"Right! Your destiny awaits!" I replied, feeling like a motivational speaker on a caffeine high.

As we walked to her department, I noticed she was biting her lip, a sure sign of her nerves. "You know, if I don't get this, I might just open a coffee shop instead," she joked.

"Only if you name it 'Prakriti's Brew-tiful Beans'!" I shot back, trying to lighten the mood. "I'll be your first customer, of course, because who wouldn't want coffee from the brilliant PhD dropout?"

"Ha! You'd have to pay full price," she teased, a grin breaking through her anxiety.

We reached her department, and when it was her turn, I held her hand and said, "I know you can do it. Best of luck!" I could see the fire of determination in her eyes—she was ready to conquer.

"Thank you so much, Gaurav," she said with that smile that could light up the entire universe (or at least my dim little corner of it).

As she walked into the interview room, I was left outside, pacing like a caged animal. Forty to fifty minutes later (but who's counting?), she emerged with a smile that made my heart do a little victory dance.

"Gaurav! I think it went well!" she exclaimed, practically glowing.

I felt like a proud parent who just watched their child win the spelling bee. "Told you! You crushed it!" I said, doing an awkward little happy dance that probably looked more like a seizure.

"Stop! You're embarrassing me!" she laughed, and oh, how I wished I could bottle that laughter and keep it forever.

"I can't help it! I'm just so happy!" I said, catching my breath. "You're officially Dr. Prakriti in my book!"

We decided to celebrate with ice cream, because nothing says "you nailed your interview" like an overflowing bowl of sugary happiness. As we sat down, I playfully suggested, "So, what's the first thing you'll do with your PhD?"

"Probably save the world," she replied, rolling her eyes dramatically. "But first, I need to figure out how to pronounce 'dichotomous' without sounding like a complete fool."

"Don't worry, I'll be your hype man," I said, pretending to hold a microphone. "Ladies and gentlemen, presenting the PhD candidate who can pronounce 'dichotomous' and still eat ice cream at the same time!"

We laughed, and for a moment, everything felt perfect. But then I caught myself thinking about how I wanted to say something more. Something that felt as big as the world, but my mouth felt like it was filled with ice cream.

"Hey, Prakriti," I began, hesitating. "I really—"

Suddenly, my phone buzzed with a notification, breaking my train of thought. "Oh, hold that thought!" I said, glancing at my phone. "It's just a reminder to feed Hardy. You know, my turtle?"

"Right! You better not neglect him," she teased. "He'll start plotting revenge."

"Yeah, he's already on the lookout for a good shell-shocking moment," I quipped. "But really, I was trying to say—"

Just then, her phone buzzed, and she answered it. I sighed, my grand moment foiled again. But hey, life has a funny way of interrupting the dramatic speeches, doesn't it?

As we finished our ice cream, I looked at her and thought, maybe next time I'd have the courage. After all, what's a little ice cream in the face of true love?

11
Brewing Confessions

A call from Prakriti flashed on my screen, and I eagerly picked it up, practically buzzing with anticipation. "I have been enrolled in the PhD program!" Her voice sparkled with joy, and I could almost hear the confetti pop in the background.

"Congratulations, Dr. Prakriti!" I exclaimed, channeling my inner game show host. "I always knew you'd make it—because let's be honest, who wouldn't want a PhD in being fabulous?"

Her laughter danced through the phone, and I could practically picture her grinning like she just won a lifetime supply of ice cream. "So when are you shifting to Gauhati University?" I asked, curious about our imminent cafe adventures.

"Maybe next week," she replied, and I could hear the excitement bubbling beneath her calm exterior.

"Dr. Prakriti, I've just gained a partner in caffeine-fueled escapades!" I announced dramatically, looking at Hardy, my turtle, who seemed to join in the celebration by splashing water around his tank. "Even Hardy is thrilled! He's practically throwing a water party!"

"Is he trying to drown himself in joy?" she quipped back, and we both burst into laughter.

"Let's just say he's not exactly the best swimmer, but his enthusiasm is off the charts," I replied, shaking my head at my pet's latest antics. "But seriously, I'm so happy for you! Now we can brainstorm all those groundbreaking research ideas over lattes—assuming you don't get too lost in your notes and forget about the actual drinking part."

"Just make sure you don't spill coffee on my research proposal!" she laughed, and I could hear the warmth in her voice.

"Noted! I'll keep my clumsiness in check. But no promises on the ice cream—once I see a sundae, all bets are off!" I winked at the phone, even though I knew she couldn't see me.

As we chatted, my heart raced a little faster. I loved her, and she didn't even know it yet. Each laugh felt like a secret promise I was too chicken to voice, but in that moment, I was just thrilled to see her happy.

And the day finally came—the one I had been eagerly anticipating—Prakriti officially shifted to Guwahati! She was allotted a room in the university itself, and let me tell you, it felt like the universe was throwing us a reunion party. I mean, who needs a PhD when you can feel this euphoric? It was like winning the lottery, but instead of money, I got my favorite person back.

Hell yeah! It was just like the old days. We'd hop onto my trusty steed—or as I liked to call it, our bat-mobile—and set off on adventures to cafes and other unexplored places around the city. Each day felt like a new chapter in an epic comic book. I was the happiest person in the world, and honestly, it felt like I had been selected for my own PhD program in happiness.

Mornings became our special time. I would visit her early for morning tea—or sometimes coffee if I was feeling particularly rebellious. There's something about caffeine that fuels both the brain and the heart, right?

"I feel so lucky to have you back again, Prakriti," I said one sunny morning, my heart doing a little jig in my chest.

"I really missed you a lot," she replied, her smile lighting up the room like a thousand suns. It was one of those moments where I wanted to freeze time—like, can someone get a photographer here?

But amidst all the joy, I still lacked the courage to propose. It felt like standing on the edge of a diving board, peering into the deep end of my feelings while my heart whispered, "Just jump!" Yet, fear kept me rooted to the spot, staring at the water, wondering if I'd sink or swim. Would she see me as more than a friend? Would she think I was just being dramatic?

My mind was racing with all these "what ifs," but in the meantime, I was content to cherish every moment with her. The adventures, the laughter, the shared coffees—all of it felt like a step closer to something deeper, something more. Who needs a PhD when you can earn a doctorate in connection?

And so, we continued our little escapades, sipping our drinks and pretending that life was perfectly scripted. Because let's be real: if life were a movie, I'd be waiting for that romantic twist where I finally found the courage to say what was in my heart. Until then, I'd happily take my seat in the audience—right next to my leading lady.

And so, a year passed in this delightful haze of coffee dates and shared laughter. With each passing day, our bond grew stronger, like a finely aged cheese—yes, I went there. But despite all the joy and camaraderie, I still hadn't mustered the courage to share my feelings with her.

Prakriti was stunning—like, drop-dead gorgeous—and I couldn't shake the thought that she probably had admirers lining up around the block, each armed with roses and cheesy pickup lines. Yet, she chose to stick with me. It felt like we had some unbreakable connection, a magnetic pull that defied the laws of physics—or at least my understanding of them. I mean, we spent hours talking about everything and nothing, and I couldn't help but feel like there was something more brewing beneath the surface.

But still, the words just wouldn't come. It was as if my heart had decided to go on a permanent vacation, leaving me to grapple with all this bottled-up emotion. I knew I had to propose—I had to bring more courage to my heart.

"C'mon, Gaurav," I'd tell myself during my morning pep talks. "It's just a few words! Just blurt it out like a toddler saying they don't like broccoli."

And yet, every time I saw her beautiful smile, my mind would short-circuit, and I'd resort to some hilarious banter instead. "So, Prakriti, have you ever considered starting a petition to declare coffee as a food group? Because I'm all in!"

She'd laugh, and I'd feel a sense of accomplishment, but deep down, I knew I was avoiding the real conversation.

Then there were those quiet moments when we'd sit together, and I could almost hear my heart whispering, "This is the moment!" But my nerves would kick in, and I'd imagine an elaborate scenario where I'd trip over my words and accidentally propose to her pet turtle instead—"Will you marry me, Hardy?"

So, there I was, stuck in my internal tug-of-war, knowing I had to take that leap but afraid of the plunge. Meanwhile, every day felt like I was living in a rom-com without the climactic confession scene. But I promised myself that I wouldn't let fear win. After all, how could I let the chance for something beautiful slip through my fingers? It was time to turn my heart's whispers into a shout.

Note from the Writer:*Ah, the chapter where Gaurav almost grows a backbone, but instead of confessing his love, he decides to keep perfecting his comedic timing. If you're wondering why he hasn't proposed yet—it's not because he's waiting for the perfect moment, he's waiting for an epiphany... or maybe just a caffeine overdose. Meanwhile, Hardy the turtle has officially accepted zero proposals so far, but stay tuned. Spoiler alert: Love and lattes are brewing.*

12
Under the Winter Streetlight

So the days turned into weeks, weeks into months, and—boom—suddenly Prakriti and I had been in this unspoken almost-relationship for over a year. Yep, one full year of friendship, coffee, late-night talks, and me awkwardly pretending I don't want more. In my head, I've tried countless times to make this ship sail into the "relationship" sea, but let me tell you, I've crashed it on the shores of awkwardness more times than I can count.

Every Sunday, we go on what I call our "unofficial dates"—though it's more like a casual coffee session where I mentally rehearse proposing for the 786th time. The rest of the week? She's lost in her research world, while I'm over here, trying not to get lost in her smile. Sometimes, she visits my apartment to hang out with Hardy, who, by the way, has now become my unlicensed love therapist. Our bond has grown so much, but my fear of ruining everything keeps my lips sealed.

But today? Today is *the day*. The day I finally muster up the courage to propose to Prakriti. I've rehearsed the speech so many times that I'm basically ready to give a TED Talk titled, "How Not to Propose to Your Crush After One Year of Epic Failures." I've tried it in front of the mirror, in front of Hardy, and even while brushing my teeth. And trust me, Hardy's judging me hard at this point. He's been giving me that look, like, "Dude, just propose already. I've seen enough of your drama."

So yeah, I'm feeling pumped, nervous, and borderline adrenaline junkie-level hyped. Red Bull should sponsor this proposal—it's *that* intense. I've overdosed on caffeine, my speech is locked and loaded, and Hardy has officially peer-pressured me into action.

I've planned everything down to the tiniest detail. Fancy restaurant? Check. Best table for two in all of Guwahati? Check. Candlelight, romantic music, perfect setting? Triple check. I've even rehearsed the entire sequence with the restaurant staff. Everyone's in on my mission except, of course, Prakriti.

I text her: "Hi, you up, Dr.? Get ready for a surprise. We're going somewhere amazing tonight."

She replies an hour later, "Sorry, I was in the shower and then went to the canteen."

(Note to self: Romantic text vs. casual canteen update—*still winning*.)

"What time?" she asks.

"Evening. Be ready by 5:00 PM," I reply, my nerves jangling like a wind chime in a hurricane.

Her response comes quick, "Okay, see you at the University gate at 5."

Alright, game on. She has no idea what's about to go down. Meanwhile, Hardy is giving me his typical "don't screw this up" look as I gear up for the night.

Evening comes. I'm in my best black suit, doused in cologne I bought specifically for this moment. Hardy gives me one final approving splash, and I head out on my trusty batmobile. My heart? Racing like I'm about to take the stage at a comedy club with no punchlines ready.

I arrive at the University gate, and there she is—Prakriti, in a stunning red dress that would make any romantic lead in a Bollywood movie jealous. Her hair is curled, and she's wearing a shade of lipstick that says, "I am the main character tonight." I almost choke on my nervous energy.

"You look... really beautiful," I stammer, and she blushes like a scene straight out of a rom-com. "Is something special happening today?" she asks, eyeing my suit with a raised eyebrow and that mischievous smile I can never get enough of.

Cue panic mode: Did she figure out my plan? Are she and Hardy secretly telepathic? Should I abandon ship and go back to being "just friends" forever?

"Nah, just felt like dressing up," I reply, trying to act cool. Spoiler alert: I am *not* cool right now. She hops onto my bike, and now there's no turning back. The mission is officially a go, and my stomach feels like it's hosting the Olympics for butterflies.

Note from the Writer:*Ah, Gaurav. Our reluctant Romeo. Watching him nervously suit up is like watching a toddler prepare for a job interview—adorable, but you know it's going to be a mess. If you're wondering why he's overdosed on caffeine, it's because he's finally this close to confessing his love... maybe. Also, if you think Hardy is just a pet turtle, think again. He's practically Gaurav's life coach at this point, probably plotting his own spin-off show while Gaurav fumbles his way through romance.*

Stay tuned. Will Gaurav manage to pop the question, or will we end up with another "almost-proposal"? Hardy's betting on the latter.

She hopped on the bike behind me, and off we went, zipping through the winter streets of Guwahati. I could feel her warmth through my jacket as she held on to me, the soft hum of the city fading into the background as I tried to focus on anything other than the fact that *tonight* could be *the night.* Or maybe not. Maybe I'd chicken out again.

The restaurant I booked was one of those candle-lit places that screamed "I have something important to say." Yeah, subtle, right? But hey, go big or go home! I'd spent hours plotting this—music, ambiance, even the moment when the dessert would arrive (because nothing says "I love you" like cheesecake, am I right?).

When we arrived, Prakriti raised an eyebrow. "Wow, this place is... fancy."

I cleared my throat. "You deserve the best." Not bad, Gaurav. Smooth.

As we stepped inside, I could already feel the butterflies in my stomach doing a full gymnastics routine. The waiter guided us to our table—right near a window overlooking the street below, twinkling with winter lights. It was romantic enough to make even the toughest guy melt a little.

We ordered, and conversation flowed like it always did—effortlessly, full of her laughter, which was the best sound in the world. But every now and then, there'd be a pause, and I'd catch her looking at me, like she knew there was more to this night. Or maybe that was just me, overthinking everything as usual.

The waiter brought out the food, and we dove into it like we hadn't eaten in days. Halfway through my plate of pasta,

I considered blurting it out right then and there. "Prakriti, I—" But then she made a joke about my sauce-covered face, and we both burst into laughter. Not exactly the moment for a heartfelt confession, huh?

As the night wore on, I could feel the weight of what I *wanted* to say pressing harder on my chest. The proposal speech I'd rehearsed a million times was dancing on the tip of my tongue, just waiting for the right moment. But every time I opened my mouth to speak, something stopped me. Fear, mostly. What if it changed everything? What if I lost her, the way she was now—my partner in crime, my cafe companion, my confidante?

By the time dessert arrived—yes, it was cheesecake—I still hadn't mustered the courage to propose. She smiled at me as she took her first bite, and I could've sworn that smile was laced with every reason I loved her. But instead of confessing, I picked up my spoon and joined her in silence. Because in that moment, just being there with her, laughing over dessert, it felt like enough.

"Gaurav?" she asked, her voice soft. "Is something on your mind?"

My heart leapt into my throat. "Uh, no! I mean, yes... but no... it's just—" I cleared my throat. "I'm just really glad you're here."

She looked at me with those eyes again, and for a split second, I thought maybe—just maybe—she was waiting for me to say more. But instead, she just smiled and took another bite of cheesecake.

Note from the writer: *Yeah, I know what you're thinking. "Gaurav, dude, just say it already!" Trust me, I'm yelling at him too. But hey, love stories aren't written in one chapter, right? Sometimes you've got to let the suspense build, let the awkwardness simmer, and—okay, okay, I'll stop. But really,* *stay tuned. You won't want to miss what happens next. Spoiler alert: there's more cheesecake.*

We stepped out of the restaurant, and I couldn't help but silently curse myself. I had planned everything, *everything*, down to the last detail—and yet, nothing had happened. No grand confession, no sweeping declaration of love, just me, Prakriti, and an evening of nervous small talk. Great job, Gaurav, really. A+ for effort, F for execution.

Prakriti climbed onto the back of my bike, and we started off into the cool winter night. It felt like one of those nostalgic moments from the past when we'd ride around aimlessly, the wind chilly but refreshing. Only tonight, something felt different. She was holding on to me a little more tightly, sitting a bit closer. I felt a warm sense of calm, but at the same time, there was that nervous fluttering in my chest, the same one that had stopped me from confessing to her a million times before.

I couldn't lose her, that was the truth. And that's what scared me. Every time I thought about saying those three words, my brain screamed, *But what if you lose her?* And so, like the perfectly rational human that I am, I made another split-second decision to delay my grand confession. Because why risk it all, right?

Then, as if by divine intervention (or maybe just impulsive panic), I pulled the bike over near the Brahmaputra River. The air was fresh and crisp, and the mist from the river added an almost magical vibe to the evening. *Alright, Gaurav, this is your moment. Don't blow it.*

"Prakriti, let's take a walk," I suggested, trying to sound casual, though I'm sure my voice betrayed every single nerve in my body.

"Sure," she said, hopping off the bike with that effortless grace she always had. We walked side by side along the riverbank. It was quiet, peaceful. A few runners passed by, some people sat near the river, but mostly, it was just us and the soft glow of the streetlights reflecting off the water.

I noticed she was shivering a bit, so like any true gentleman, I took off my jacket and gave it to her. Yes, I know, it was a classic move—but hey, it worked.

The silence between us wasn't uncomfortable; it was… nice. Comfortable. We had these moments often, where words weren't really necessary. Still, there was something in the air tonight, something unspoken that felt like it was waiting to burst. The winter cold was nipping at my skin, but inside, my heart was practically doing somersaults.

And then, I had a flashback.

It hit me like a truck: that day in Tezpur, the first time we walked together by the Brahmaputra. It was eerily similar. The jacket, the river, the way she looked at me—it was all the same. It was like I had gone back in time. Time really did fly, didn't it? Except this time, I wasn't just a clueless idiot. Well, I was *still* a clueless idiot, but tonight was going to be different.

I slowed down, trailing a bit behind her, lost in my thoughts. Then, without thinking, I just blurted it out.

"Prakriti," I called out softly.

She stopped, turned to face me, standing just under the soft glow of a streetlight. Her face was framed perfectly by the light, her smile soft and radiant, and I swear, in that moment, time slowed down. The mist curled gently around us, and the streetlight seemed to halo her face. It was perfect. Too perfect. *This is it, Gaurav. You can't mess this up.*

"I… I… la… I love you, Prakriti," I stammered out, feeling like I had just thrown myself off a cliff with no parachute.

She stared at me for a second, her face unreadable. "I didn't hear that," she said, taking a step closer.

Wait. What? Did she just—was she serious? My heart did a somersault, then landed in my stomach. Was this some kind of test?

I gathered every ounce of courage I had left. "I said... I love you, Prakriti," I repeated, feeling like I was about to pass out.

"I didn't get it," she said again, taking another step closer, her smile growing wider.

Okay, now she was messing with me, right? My brain was short-circuiting. I was on the verge of tears at this point—seriously, this was emotional warfare.

I stepped closer too. Now we were only a few inches apart. I could feel her breath, see the glimmer in her eyes. This had to be the cruelest form of flirting I had ever experienced. "I love you, Prakriti," I said, my voice quieter but firm.

She looked up at me, her eyes twinkling with mischief. "Still can't hear you. Come a little closer."

I was ready to collapse right there on the spot. But I took the final step until we were nearly touching. She tilted her head slightly, her eyes locking onto mine, and I could barely breathe.

"I love you, Prakriti. I really love you," I whispered, my voice shaky but sincere.

And then, she smiled—the kind of smile that made my knees weak—and wrapped her arms around me. "I love you too, Gaurav," she said softly, her voice breaking with emotion. "I've been waiting for this day for so long."

Wait, what? Did I hear that right? My brain was scrambling to catch up. She loves me too?! I felt her hug me tighter, and I realized I wasn't dreaming. This was real.

"I thought you'd never say it," she murmured into my shoulder. "That's why I was pretending not to hear. I wanted to mess with you a bit."

I laughed, a mix of relief and disbelief. "You've been torturing me all this time?"

She pulled back slightly, looking into my eyes. "Well, you deserved it. Why did you take so long?"

"I was afraid... afraid of losing you," I admitted.

Her expression softened as she cupped my face in her hands. "You'll never lose me, Gaurav. Never."

And before I knew it, our lips met. It wasn't some Hollywood-style, dramatic kiss. It was warm, soft, and perfect. Her arms wrapped tighter around me, and I held her close, under the streetlight, with the mist swirling around us.

We stood there for what felt like an eternity, lost in each other.

"I love you, Gaurav," she said again, her voice barely a whisper.

"I love you too, Prakriti," I replied, my voice catching as I blinked back tears. This was real. She was real. We were real.

As we rode back on my bike, she hugged me from behind, her arms wrapped tightly around me. The cold winter wind no longer felt biting—it was warm, comforting, and perfect.

When I dropped her off at her hostel, I couldn't resist one last, "Goodnight, Prakriti. I love you."

She smiled, that same smile that had made me fall in love with her a thousand times over. "I love you too."

I handed her a small letter I'd written earlier, just in case the proposal went well. "Read this later," I said, my heart still racing.

As I rode back to my apartment, I still couldn't believe what had just happened. Was it a fairy-tale? Maybe. Or maybe some love stories are just meant to unfold like this, in their own time, at their own pace. Not perfectly, but perfectly enough.

Note from the writer: *And there it is, folks! Finally, after all the will-they-won't-they drama, they said it! I bet you're feeling relieved, huh? I know I am. Now, don't worry—I've got plenty more in store for Gaurav and Prakriti. But let's all take a moment to bask in the glow of that winter streetlight kiss, because who doesn't love a good slow-burn love story?*

13

Confessions, Cousins, and Judo Slams

The alarm blared, jolting me awake like a bucket of cold water. Was it all a dream? My mind was foggy, like when you wake up and can't quite tell if you're still in your head or in the real world. Had I really confessed my love to Prakriti? Did she actually say she loved me back, or was that just my mind messing with me again?

I sat up in bed, staring blankly at Hardy, my unofficial therapist in turtle form. His tank bubbled peacefully, as if he was in on some cosmic joke. Then, *ping*, a message popped up on my phone.

"Good morning, Gaurav. It feels like a dream, what happened yesterday."

I froze. Okay, this was real. Definitely real.

Another message: *"I was really waiting for this day for so long."*

And another: *"I love you, Gaurav. I feel like I'm on cloud nine."*

My heart did a weird flutter, like it was practicing for the Olympics. Meanwhile, Hardy splashed around in his tank like he was celebrating, practically throwing a mini turtle rave. I walked over to him, chuckling. "We did it, buddy. We really did it." Hardy blinked at me, probably wondering when he'd get his next meal, but I swear he was mentally giving me a high-five from inside that tank.

I grabbed my phone, my hands still shaky. *"I love you too, Prakriti."* My fingers danced over the keys. *"I wanted to tell you every day, but I was so scared of losing you."*

Her reply was almost immediate: *"I'll never leave you alone."*

Cue my heart doing that Olympic somersault again. I had the dumbest grin on my face, like a kid who just discovered candy grows on trees.

"Your letter touched me so much," she texted next, *"I read it over and over."*

"I'm so glad you liked it," I typed back, *"And thank YOU for being a part of my life."*

And then, her next message had me laughing out loud: *"Is Hardy okay with this? I mean, he has to share you now."*

I glanced at Hardy, who, of course, chose that exact moment to splash water everywhere like he was trying to outshine my emotional moment. *"Yeah, he's given his official approval,"* I texted back, adding a wink emoji.

"I really love you, Gaurav," she wrote, *"I was waiting for this for so long."*

"Everything happens for a reason," I replied, grinning like an idiot. *"I was destined to crash-land into your life."*

I swear, I could feel her smiling through the screen. My mind flashed back to last night—her breath so close, our kiss under the streetlight. It all felt surreal, like a scene straight out of a movie, except it was my life. (I mean, if Hardy had popcorn, he'd be watching this unfold like a Netflix rom-com.)

"Gaurav, gotta go now. My guide just texted me, calling me in for research. Love you!"

"Good luck, Dr. Prakriti," I replied. *"I love you too."*

I put my phone down and looked at Hardy. He just blinked slowly at me, like he had known this all along.

"I told you, bro," I imagined him saying, in his slow, turtle-y wisdom. "She loves you. You just never listen."

I laughed, sitting back on my bed. Hardy was right. Maybe all this time, I should've trusted the turtle.

Note from the writer: *Well, folks, here we are! Gaurav finally got his girl, and Hardy—our unsung hero—gets to enjoy the sweet taste of victory (or at least some well-deserved turtle pellets). I'm sure you're just as relieved as I am that we didn't have to wait another year for this to happen. Stay tuned for more heart-melting moments and, of course, Hardy's wise yet silent support in the background.*

So, the days flew by in a whirlwind of coffee dates, cheeky texts, and the honeymoon phase that felt like we were walking on clouds. You know that feeling, right? The kind where everything seems brighter, every text makes your heart do a backflip, and even the most mundane moments feel like magic. Yeah, that's exactly how it was with Prakriti. Oh, and did I mention? I officially have a girlfriend! I mean, *finally*. Yes, universe, thank you for aligning those stars.

I still can't believe how this all started. Our first awkward meeting at a café, our mutual friends introducing us, and eventually those "unofficial" dates—each one more nerve-wracking than the last. And here we are now, living in this romantic movie I'm still half-convinced I'm dreaming. Everything felt surreal, like I was one step away from someone pulling a "Truman Show" on me.

Fast forward to last weekend: Prakriti and I were out shopping at the mall. Casual, right? Except for the fact that she looked like she'd just stepped out of a movie premiere. White dress, bangles, heels—yeah, I was that guy walking next to an angel who just happened to be casually flipping through books like it was no big deal.

So there we were, wandering through a bookstore on the top floor of the mall. Prakriti, glasses on, hair flowing, was completely absorbed in the bookshelves. And me? Well, I was somewhere between pretending to care about book blurbs and stealing glances at her. But then, out of nowhere—cue dramatic music—a guy came swooping in like he was on a mission to ruin my day. He straight-up *snatched* the book out of Prakriti's hands and started laughing like he was auditioning for the role of "Mall Villain #1."

I froze. Was this guy serious? My brain short-circuited for a moment, and before I could even register what was happening, he was walking toward me, still laughing and teasing her. And that's when something snapped. A sudden, uncontrollable *Dragon Ball Z* moment overtook me. Yep, I went full Super Saiyan. My hands acted on their own, and before I knew it, I had thrown this guy in a perfect *seoi-nage* (a judo throw, for the uninitiated). Boom! He hit the ground, out cold.

People started gathering, murmuring to each other like they were watching an impromptu martial arts demo. I, meanwhile, was standing there like a proud action hero in my own mind—until Prakriti came running over, yelling the guy's name.

Wait... *what*?

"Niku! Niku!" She was shaking him, tears in her eyes. Oh no. Oh no, no, no. This is not good.

Niku—who, by the way, had just been *judo-slammed* by yours truly—opened his eyes groggily, looked at Prakriti, and said in the weakest voice ever, "Di Di..."

Di Di? My mind was spinning. Did this guy just call her *sister?*

I stammered like an idiot. "Prakriti, do you... know him?" I asked, voice trembling like a kid who just got caught breaking a vase.

"He's my cousin brother, Niku," she replied, eyes still glistening with tears. I swear, my stomach dropped through the floor and straight into the basement.

And there I was, standing like a statue, mouth dry, heart in my shoes, trying to process what had just happened. Prakriti's cousin was now the victim of my overzealous judo throw. Great. What an epic start to this relationship.

Niku, still lying on the ground, smiled weakly. "I'm fine, Di Di. It's all a misunderstanding."

Yeah, understatement of the century, buddy.

"I have this playful nature, you know? I get why you reacted that way," he added, sitting up slowly.

I couldn't believe what I'd done. I had just *seoi-nage-ed* my girlfriend's cousin—on our first official date. Seriously, where's my award for "Most Epic Fail"? Gryffindor may have gained ten points, but I had lost all my dignity.

As I helped Niku up, I muttered, "I'm so sorry, man. It was a misunderstanding. I thought you were, you know... a creep." Smooth, Gaurav. Real smooth.

"You're strong, brother-in-law!" Niku said with a shaky grin, giving me an awkward thumbs-up.

Oh great. Now I'm "brother-in-law." Just bury me now.

Prakriti, still shaken, gave me this look—half sympathy, half "what have you done?"—and said, "Don't worry. It's all fine. Niku's fine." Her voice calmed me, but inside, I was still a mess.

And then, like the true comedian he was, Niku chimed in, "I was actually here to surprise you guys, but... surprise, I got thrown!" He let out a weak laugh. "Talk about an UNO reverse card."

We finally left the bookstore with Prakriti's selection of books—though the real story wasn't the titles she picked, but the epic takedown that happened right in front of them. We headed to the food court, people giving us confused looks, probably thinking, "Weren't those three just in a fight? Why are they having lunch together now?"

As we sat down to eat, Niku turned to me, still munching on fries. "So, I heard you have a turtle named Hardy?"

I sighed, trying to regain some dignity. "Yeah, Hardy's famous in his own right. You should come by and meet him sometime."

We ate, we laughed, and Prakriti spent most of the time teasing her brother, while I prayed to the universe that I hadn't just messed up my new relationship. "Don't worry," she said at one point, noticing my guilt. "He's fine. Really."

Niku nodded. "Yeah, you're alright, Gaurav. Just, you know, maybe no judo next time."

I grinned sheepishly, "I'll keep that in mind."

As the day wrapped up and we parted ways, I couldn't help but laugh at the ridiculousness of it all. First date with my girlfriend, and I threw her cousin in a mall. If there was a manual for how to *not* date, I was officially the poster boy.

Note for the writer: *Well, that escalated quickly! Gaurav, our lovable judo master, somehow managed to turn his first official date into an episode of WWE Smackdown. Lucky for him, Prakriti's a trooper (and her brother's apparently got a sense of humor). Lesson of the day? Don't mess with a guy's* *girlfriend—even if you're her cousin. Also, maybe Hardy should take over the dating advice next time. Stay tuned!*

14

Anniversary Bliss: A Recipe for Love

Hurry! It's our anniversary today! It feels just like the day I first met Prakriti. You know, the awkwardness, the shy glances, the awkward jokes that only I found funny—ah, the good ol' days! But look at us now, thriving in our relationship, and I'm about to pull off the most epic Hollywood-style proposal on this special day. I can already picture it: our first kiss on the bridge under the streetlight, where time stood still.

Right now, she's lying next to me with her eyes closed, her hair cascading over her cheeks like a scene from a romantic movie. I swear, she looks so beautiful, it's like I'm watching a nature documentary, and the narrator is saying, "And here we see the rare Prakriti in her natural habitat."

Of course, I should probably mention that she's been giving her research paper a run for its money. Papers, journals, sticky notes—it's like a paper explosion went off in our apartment. And let me tell you, this isn't just an apartment anymore; it's a home filled with our shared dreams, caffeinated chaos, and Hardy, our turtle, who now has the dubious honor of being Prakriti's unofficial research assistant.

Speaking of Hardy, he's been totally spoiled by Prakriti. The little guy gets fed whenever he gives her that adorable look, which is often. I mean, who can resist that face? So, big shoutout to Hardy for his contribution to our relationship—he's practically the MVP around here.

As she sleeps, I'm just sitting here watching her, taking in how peaceful she looks. It's like she knows she's safe around me. I lean down and kiss her forehead, breathing in the sweet scent of her hair. "I love you, babe," I whisper before tiptoeing out of bed.

I head to the kitchen to make our coffee. Let's face it: we're caffeine addicts at this point. I whip up a breakfast spread complete with a red rose on the tray, a small teddy bear, and a bunch of chocolates—because what's an anniversary without a little sugar rush? Hardy gets some food too because, you know, "happy turtle, happy life."

As I return to the bedroom, I see her still sleeping soundly. I gently move her papers and laptop to the side so I can place the breakfast tray beside her. Then, I wrap my arms around her and kiss her softly on the lips.

"Happy anniversary, babe," I say as she slowly blinks awake, and her smile lights up the room like a thousand suns.

"Happy anniversary, love!" she replies, and we share another kiss—one that could rival any romantic film. Then, I notice her eyes dart to the side table, where she spots the rose, letter, and teddy bear. She gets all teary-eyed, and my heart melts.

"Gaurav, you're going to make me cry!" she exclaims, pulling me in for another hug. "You always know how to make me feel special with your gifts and letters. They're like little love bombs that explode right into my heart."

"I can do anything for you, Prakriti," I say, trying not to get too mushy. But let's be real, mushy is my middle name right now.

She takes the rose and inhales deeply. "This is the luckiest rose ever!" she says, her eyes glimmering as she unfolds my letter. I'm just here, casually feeding her breakfast, feeling like the world's most devoted boyfriend.

"I'm so touched by your letters, Gaurav," she reads, and I can see the tears glistening in her eyes. "You always make me feel like I'm the star of the show!"

And I'm over here thinking, "Who needs a reality TV show when we have this?" But I keep that thought to myself because, let's face it, the last thing I need is a camera crew following us around while we do our daily coffee runs.

As she resumes her research work, I'm just happily feeding her breakfast like some kind of modern-day prince charming. "You know, I'm pretty sure I'm going to need a PhD in breakfast-making soon," I joke, grabbing a bite of her crispy honey chicken wings while pretending to offer her a bite.

"Look at you, being all supportive," she laughs, playfully swatting my hand away.

"Just doing my part, you know? Plus, I need to keep up with all these research proposals you're going to be throwing at me. 'Dear Gaurav, I propose we research the effects of too much caffeine on our love lives...'"

"Careful, or I might just make that a real study!" she quips back, her eyes sparkling with mischief.

Honestly, these moments are everything to me. Each laugh, each bite of food, and every little glance shared—it all feels like a perfectly written love story, even if I can't quite figure out the plot just yet. I just know I want to be with her, forever.

And so, as we sit together, laughing over breakfast and dreaming about the future, I can't help but think: Who needs the perfect script when you have the perfect partner?

Note from the writer: *Ah, the sweet taste of love and breakfast—what a combination! If you thought this chapter was just about a romantic breakfast, think again! It's about a guy finally realizing he's on a lifelong adventure with the woman of his dreams, all while juggling turtle responsibilities. Stay tuned for more awkward moments, love declarations, and maybe a judo throw or two, because let's face it, nothing in Gaurav's life ever goes according to plan!*

15
Romance in the Rearview

As our romance continued to blossom, one day we both managed to get a day off, which is as rare as Hardy skipping a meal. So, naturally, we decided it was the perfect time for a mini holiday. We packed our lunch, sorted everything for the trip, and made sure Hardy's automatic feeder was loaded—because, let's be honest, Hardy is the real king of this household, with his unlimited buffet whenever we're not around.

Prakriti, as always, looked absolutely fabulous in her sundress, with those oversized sunglasses and a big floppy hat that gave off serious Audrey Hepburn vibes. Meanwhile, I, the man of impeccable (read: mostly black) fashion sense, had—thanks to the grace of Prakriti—added some color to my wardrobe. Today, I was sporting a pink T-shirt and gray pants. Yeah, I know. *Pink?* But hey, when Prakriti picks your outfit and says you look good, who's there to judge? Plus, she quite literally brought color into my life—and my wardrobe. All I needed was her approval, and I was good to go.

"You ready, babe?" I asked, leaning in for a quick kiss, which I knew would be my fuel for the day. Who needs Red

Bull when you've got love?

"Ready to roll!" she replied with a grin that could power a city.

Of course, I felt a little bad leaving Hardy behind, but we couldn't break the rules by triple-sitting on a bike. Plus, the guy doesn't even have a helmet! Sorry, buddy, you're staying behind this time. Though, let's be real—he doesn't care as long as his automatic feeder is loaded. I could almost hear Hardy thinking, *"You guys have fun, I've got an all-you-can-eat buffet right here."*

With that, we set off for Kaziranga, chasing the nostalgia of our first trip together. It was a long drive from Guwahati, but it didn't matter. It's been over a year since our anniversary, and trips like this were rare, especially with Prakriti's PhD research keeping her busy. And let's not forget, I work from home—living the *software developer dream*—which, if you remember, means I once had no life outside of coding. But now, with her by my side, life had more color than my old all-black wardrobe days.

As we hit the road, the wind blowing through Prakriti's hair, I couldn't help but smile at how much my life had changed. From endless lines of code to road trips with the girl of my dreams, and yes, a turtle who eats like a king.

Note from the Writer: *Yep, Gaurav's come a long way—from colorless clothes and a life spent staring at a computer screen to planning spontaneous trips with his dream girl. And if you're wondering how Hardy feels about all of this, don't worry. The only thing Hardy cares about is food. Lots and lots of food.*

As we approached the resort, I couldn't help but feel a mix of excitement and nerves. I mean, who wouldn't be a little jittery planning a surprise for someone as incredible as Prakriti? Not to mention that the resort was her dream destination, and I had just managed to pull off what felt like an extravagant feat of romantic wizardry. I felt like I should be wearing a cape or something—"Gaurav the Great, Master of Surprises!"

"Wow, this place is beautiful!" Prakriti exclaimed as we stepped onto the property, her eyes sparkling with wonder.

"Just wait until you see what's inside," I said, trying to keep my tone casual while my heart was doing somersaults. She had no idea what was coming, and I was practically bursting with excitement.

We parked the bike, and as I held her hand, I could feel her curiosity radiating off her like the sun. "Where are we going?" she asked, a slight frown creasing her forehead as she tried to piece together the puzzle that was my plan.

"Just a little surprise," I said, leading her toward the dining hall. "Trust me; you're going to love it."

"I'm not sure if I should be excited or scared," she joked, glancing at me sideways. "You know how you get with surprises. Remember the 'spontaneous' trip to the roadside tea stall that turned into a near-death experience?"

I chuckled, shaking my head. "That was a one-time thing! This is different, I promise. No potholes or cows involved. Just pure romance, minus the chaos."

"Fingers crossed," she replied, still a little skeptical but grinning. I could feel her excitement building as we walked closer to the entrance.

When we entered the dining hall, the first thing she noticed was the elegant table set for two, adorned with beautiful flowers and flickering candles. Her eyes went wide, and her jaw dropped. "Gaurav... what is all this?"

I grinned, trying to play it cool. "Well, I thought we could celebrate our anniversary in style. You know, just a casual dinner at a place that costs more than my life savings."

"Wait, did you actually book the entire dining hall?" she asked, her voice rising in disbelief.

"Um, maybe?" I shrugged, trying to act nonchalant while my inner self was doing backflips. "I mean, it's not every day I get to celebrate with the love of my life."

"I can't believe you did all this for me!" she said, her eyes shimmering with gratitude. "You're too much, Gaurav!"

I laughed, holding up my hands defensively. "Hey, don't put me on a pedestal. I just really wanted to surprise you! Plus, I had to redeem myself after the pothole incident."

As we sat down at the table, I poured her a glass of sparkling wine, because let's be real: nothing says romance like fancy wine. "Cheers to surprises!" I said, raising my glass.

"Cheers to you, Mr. Smooth Operator," she laughed, clinking her glass against mine. "This is amazing."

The food started to arrive, and I made sure to order all of her favorites. As the plates came, I noticed she was just staring at everything, mouth agape. "I don't know what to say!" she exclaimed, looking genuinely overwhelmed.

"Say 'thank you' and eat, woman!" I teased, grinning at her. "I'm not a chef, but I promise I didn't burn anything this time."

"Gaurav, I really don't deserve this," she said, shaking her head in disbelief.

"Wrong! You absolutely do deserve this and more. You bring so much joy into my life. Plus, I owe you for the 'almost dropping the bike' moment. This is just me saying I appreciate you—now eat!"

She laughed and dug into the food, and I couldn't help but smile as I watched her enjoy every bite. "I swear you have a sixth sense for finding the best places," she said between mouthfuls.

"I might have consulted some reviews and asked a few locals," I admitted sheepishly. "Okay, fine, I used Google Maps and read all the reviews like a responsible adult."

"Next thing you know, you'll be giving me a TED Talk on the art of planning surprises," she teased, her eyes dancing with mischief.

"Only if you promise to attend, front row seat and all," I replied, leaning in conspiratorially. "I'll even throw in free snacks."

As the evening continued and we polished off the delicious meal, I could see the excitement growing in Prakriti's eyes. She was radiant, and I couldn't help but feel like the luckiest guy in the universe. But hold on—there was one more surprise waiting to be unveiled, and I was practically bursting at the seams to reveal it.

"Alright, babe," I said, leaning in closer with a conspiratorial grin. "There's one last surprise for tonight."

Her eyebrows shot up, curiosity dancing in her gaze. "Another surprise? Gaurav, you're killing me with all this suspense!"

I chuckled, trying to maintain an air of mystery. "Just trust me on this one. Are you ready to see your next surprise?"

"I'm ready!" she exclaimed, a hint of nervous excitement in her voice.

I took her hand and led her out of the dining hall, my heart racing with anticipation. As we stepped outside, the warm night air enveloped us. I led her toward a separate entrance, where the resort staff awaited, holding a beautiful bouquet of flowers and beaming smiles.

"Welcome to your deluxe room!" one of them said, gesturing for us to enter.

When we walked in, Prakriti gasped. The room was transformed into a romantic wonderland. There were candles flickering softly on every surface, casting a warm, inviting glow. Balloons floated cheerfully around the room, and a delicious cake sat on the table, decorated to perfection.

"Gaurav... this is incredible!" she gasped, taking it all in.

"But wait, there's more!" I added, giving her a playful nudge. "Look at the walls!"

She turned to see that the walls were adorned with photos from our time together—pictures from our first bike ride, our goofy faces at that tea stall, and even a candid shot of her laughing at something I said (which is a rare treasure, trust me).

"Is that... our entire journey?" she asked, tears glistening in her eyes. "You've captured all of this?"

"Yep! Just a little something to remind you of all the adventures we've had together."

"Gaurav, this is beyond amazing," she said, her voice filled with emotion. "I can't believe you went to all this trouble!"

"And there's still more," I said, motioning toward the table laden with chocolates—so many chocolates that it looked like Willy Wonka himself had set up shop in our room. "Because what's a celebration without an excessive amount of chocolate?"

"You really thought of everything!" she said, grinning from ear to ear. "I feel like a princess!"

"Well, you are my princess," I replied with a wink. "And every princess deserves to be spoiled."

I watched as she wandered around the room, touching the flowers and taking in all the details. "Gaurav, you really outdid yourself. This is just... perfect."

"Just trying to keep the romance alive," I said, feigning nonchalance. "And besides, I wanted to make this anniversary unforgettable. So, surprise! Welcome to our romantic lair for the night!"

Prakriti laughed, and I could see the joy radiating from her. "I can't believe this. You really know how to make a girl feel special."

"Only the best for you, babe," I said, stepping closer and wrapping my arms around her. "Now, let's cut the cake, enjoy the chocolates, and celebrate us."

As we sat together, indulging in the sweet treats and surrounded by the flickering candles, I couldn't help but feel that this moment was everything I had hoped it would be.

The universe may have a wicked sense of humor, but tonight? It felt like everything had aligned perfectly.

Note from the Writer: *Surprise! Because what's a romantic getaway without enough decorations to make a wedding planner weep with joy? Gaurav really went all out to make Prakriti's anniversary unforgettable, and if that doesn't scream romance, I don't know what does. Buckle up, because this love story is only getting sweeter—just like the cake!*

As we stood there in the middle of nowhere, basking in the aftermath of our picturesque day, I suddenly blurted out, "What if our bike gets punctured?"

Classic Gaurav, right? You'd think I'd learned by now that some thoughts should stay locked away in the vault of my mind. But, nooo—my brain decided to play the "let's jinx the day" game.

And wouldn't you know it, just as I revved the engine to move on, the universe decided to take my casual remark as a challenge. Boom! Puncture. Right there, in the middle of nowhere. It was as if the bike was in cahoots with my inner monologue.

"Congratulations, Gaurav! You've earned yourself a flat tire!" I thought sarcastically, rolling my eyes at fate.

"Uh, so what now?" Prakriti asked, eyeing the tire as if it might sprout legs and walk away. "Are we supposed to wait for a rescue team?"

"Or a miracle," I replied, trying to sound optimistic, but internally I was already pushing my heavy bike, my muscles screaming in protest. "Maybe I should have worn my superhero cape today. That would have come in handy right about now."

As we waited, I felt a mix of dread and frustration creeping in. "Why is it that the second we decide to take a day off, we end up in an episode of 'Survivor: Bike Edition'?"

Just then, like a scene from a movie, a bike came rolling down the road. The rider, a good-looking guy, stopped to help. "Hey! You need assistance?"

"Only if you have a spare tube and a team of mechanics ready to go," I joked, trying to lighten the mood. Prakriti chuckled beside me, but my heart was still racing.

"Just 1.5 km ahead is a puncture shop," the guy said, glancing between us. "You can push your bike, and I can take your friend there. I promise she'll be back in no time."

Prakriti looked at me, and before I could say anything else, she hopped onto the back of the stranger's bike, her trust in humanity shining brighter than my anxiety. "See you at the shop!" she called back cheerfully, as I stood there feeling like a giant neon sign of bad decision-making.

"Wait, what just happened?" I muttered to myself. "Am I really pushing my bike alone while she's off with Mr. Handsome?"

Panic rushed through me as I pushed my bike faster. "What type of decision was that?" I yelled after them, but all

I got was the sound of my own voice echoing back at me.

I tried to call her, but of course, no signal. "Just great," I grumbled, huffing and puffing like a train about to derail. "I'm going to be that guy who loses his girlfriend on a simple trip because of a flat tire. Perfect. Just perfect."

I pushed my bike for what felt like an eternity, and finally, the mystery man returned without Prakriti. "Brother, it's just 500m from here! I dropped her at the puncture shop," he said, looking a little confused.

"500m?" I echoed, suddenly feeling every inch of that distance. "That sounds like a marathon to me."

I hurried to the shop, my heart pounding with a mix of worry and guilt. And then, I saw her. Relief washed over me like a tidal wave. "Prakriti!" I exclaimed, rushing over. "You're okay!"

"Of course I am!" she laughed, brushing off the tension. "We really made a dumb move, Gaurav."

"I'm so sorry! I didn't mean to jinx our trip," I replied, my voice a blend of relief and embarrassment. "I should've kept my mouth shut."

"It's okay! The moment was intense," she said with a smile, "and besides, he was a nice guy. Just don't let it happen again, okay?"

"Thank God you're safe," I muttered, and with a dramatic flourish, I thanked the universe. "If you'd been lost, I'd have been forced to do something reckless—like go on a dating app to find a replacement!"

As the puncture was fixed, I couldn't help but steal glances at Prakriti, who seemed unfazed by the chaos. "You're amazing, you know that?" I said as we watched the mechanic work.

"I try!" she replied, nudging me playfully. "Now let's get out of here before you manifest another disaster!"

With the bike finally back in working order, we set off toward home. Yes, there was a bit of sweetness mixed with the sourness of the day, but if nothing else, it made for a great story to tell later.

And let's be real—what's a love story without a few bumps in the road? Or a flat tire? Or a spontaneous mini-adventure in the middle of nowhere? So here we were, riding into the sunset, both ready for whatever the universe threw at us next.

Note from the writer : *Ah, love on the open road! Nothing screams romance quite like a flat tire in the middle of nowhere, am I right? Gaurav and Prakriti's adventure may have taken a slight detour, but isn't that what makes life exciting? It's all about the unexpected moments—like trusting a stranger with your girlfriend while you're left behind with nothing but a heavy bike and a whole lot of anxiety.And let's not forget Hardy, our not-so-great guardian of the home front. He's living the good life, munching away while our protagonists embark on their escapades. Seriously, he's probably plotting how to overthrow Gaurav as the true head of the household.So buckle up, dear readers! This love story is packed with more twists and turns than a country road, and trust me, Gaurav's mishaps are just getting started. Spoiler alert: there's plenty more chaos, laughter, and a few heartwarming moments ahead. Because what's a romantic journey without a few bumps—and maybe a pothole or two? Stay tuned for more wild adventures!*

16

Tears and Triumphs

It had been three years since Prakriti and I embarked on this beautiful rollercoaster called love, and I still couldn't shake the feeling that it was all a dream. Our home was practically a jungle of sticky notes and scattered journals—seriously, it looked like a tornado had hit an office supply store. You ask me about her thesis, and I might as well have a PhD myself; I could defend her work at this point. The day she finally gets that "Dr." title, I'll proudly claim the title of "Unofficial Dr." because let's be real, I've invested just as much into this process as she has.

I was in the living room, daydreaming about our journey together, when I heard her voice echoing through the house, laced with panic. "Gaurav!" she cried out, and I sprinted toward the sound like I was racing in the Olympics, expecting the worst.

When I reached her, my heart dropped. She was cradling Hardy in her arms, tears streaming down her face. "What is it, Prakriti?" I asked, rushing to her side.

"I think something's wrong with Hardy," she choked out, her voice trembling.

As I leaned closer, I could see Hardy—my turtle—showing only the slightest movement, his eyes shut tight. My heart shattered into a million pieces. I wrapped my arms around Prakriti, pulling her close, trying to comfort her while desperately trying not to cry myself. If I started tearing up, I feared she might lose it completely.

"He'll be okay," I said, attempting to soothe her. "We'll take him to the vet as soon as they open. I've already made an appointment."

But instead of reassurance, she just stared at me with those tear-filled eyes, and I knew my words had little effect. Watching her like this was like trying to stand strong in the middle of a hurricane. It hurt more than I could express.

After what felt like an eternity, the vet's office finally opened. We rushed Hardy in, and the doctor examined him while we waited with bated breath. I held Prakriti's hand tightly, trying to channel some positive energy, but the weight of the situation hung heavy in the air.

"Unfortunately, he's suffering from an eye infection," the doctor finally said, his tone serious. "If his eyes don't open soon, we might lose him."

I felt the world tilt beneath me. My heart sank, and I glanced at Prakriti, who had gone completely still. Tears streamed down her face as we listened to the vet explain that Hardy would need to be kept for observation. I swallowed hard, trying to maintain my composure for her sake.

When we got home, Prakriti didn't say much. She sat in front of Hardy's tank, staring blankly, as if her entire world had just crumbled. I approached her slowly, kissed her forehead, and whispered, "He'll be okay."

She didn't respond, and my heart ached for her. I wiped her tears away, but it felt like nothing I said could break through the thick fog of sadness that enveloped us.

As the hours dragged on, I headed to the kitchen, trying to keep my mind busy. That's when I noticed the stove burner pipe was loose and leaking gas. I figured I could fix it. I mean, how hard could it be? Just a quick saw with my trusty knife and—wait for it—disaster strikes.

In my enthusiasm, the knife slipped, and I felt a deep cut slice into my hand. Blood gushed out as I staggered toward the bathroom. "Of all the dumb things to do!" I thought, panic swirling in my chest. I stumbled, fainting into the bucket, crashing down like a ragdoll.

"Gaurav… Gaurav… Gaurav!" I heard a distant voice. Was that Prakriti?

"Gaurav… what happened? Gaurav!" The panic in her voice pierced through the haze.

"Gaurav… open your eyes!" I struggled to focus, my vision a blurry mess. I felt water splashed on my face and hands desperately trying to wipe the blood away.

I blinked slowly, and there she was, Prakriti, looking pale and frantic, tearing strips from her T-shirt to bind my hand. "I was so afraid," she said, her voice breaking.

"Hey, hey, I'm okay, calm down," I replied, my voice hoarse. Honestly, I was starting to feel a little lightheaded, but I couldn't let her see that. I needed to be strong for her.

As my senses returned, I noticed the bloodstains on the floor and realized I had somehow become the star of my own horror movie. "I guess I'm banned from the kitchen now, huh?" I chuckled weakly, trying to lighten the mood.

"You're definitely banned from anything that requires sharp objects," she shot back, her eyes still glistening with unshed tears. "You have to stop worrying me like this."

I smiled at her, feeling grateful she was still with me, even in this chaotic moment. "I promise to be more careful.

But can we just take a moment to acknowledge how much of a klutz I am?"

Just as we settled down to process everything, my phone rang. It was the vet's office. I held my breath, hoping for good news. "Yes?" I answered.

"Mr. Gaurav? Hardy's eyes have opened. He's going to be fine!"

I nearly dropped the phone in shock. "Really?" I couldn't believe it. I turned to Prakriti, who looked at me with wide eyes, waiting for the news.

"He's fine!" I exclaimed, and the relief washed over us both. I swept her into a hug, and we both let out a breath we hadn't realized we were holding.

After all the drama, we finally had some good news, and for the first time in days, Prakriti smiled genuinely. "You scared me, you know?" she said, pulling back to look at me.

"Trust me, I scared myself too," I replied, grinning. "But hey, look on the bright side: at least Hardy isn't planning to take his final plunge just yet!"

"Let's go get him," she said, her eyes sparkling once more, full of hope.

As we left, I held her close, knowing that this rollercoaster of emotions had only strengthened our bond. The universe had thrown us both some major curveballs, but we made it through together, and that was what mattered.

Note from the Writer*: And there you have it, folks! Just another day in the life of Gaurav and Prakriti, where romance meets sheer chaos. Who knew love could be so messy? But hey, that's what makes it all worthwhile, right? Buckle up; it's only going to get wilder from here!*

17
Chaos, Confessions, and the Ex Factor

Alright, dear reader, brace yourself. We're diving into a story that's not just a story—it's a maze of thoughts, mishaps, and outright chaos. And if you think you can just sit back and enjoy, think again. This one's going to demand a little more from you. Ready to get lost with me?

Chapter: The Great Period Panic and The Ex Conundrum

Day 1: THE PERIOD PANIC

It all started with **The Missed Period**.

Yes, *that* dreaded thing. The one that turns even the calmest souls into hyperactive anxiety monsters. It doesn't matter how logical you are—if you're 99.9% sure she's not pregnant, that 0.1% is going to have you Googling "parenting tips" at 2 AM.

And of course, *that* moment happened to us. Prakriti missed her period, and while she was calm—like **Buddha-level calm**—I was not.

I'm pacing around the house, thinking back to that one night, you know the one. The one you replay over and over in your head, like some weird glitch in the matrix. Meanwhile, what's Prakriti doing? Oh, she's chilling. Not worried at all. Like, how?!

But wait, before we get too deep into this panic, let's rewind a bit.

FLASHBACK

I'm banned from the kitchen. Yep, *banned*. Why? Well, that's another story, one involving a knife, some blood, and me almost turning our kitchen into a crime scene. Prakriti—being the loving, supportive girlfriend—now forbids me from entering that sacred space. So, here I am, trying to bring her black coffee (delivered safely to the desk this time), while she's sitting there, working on her PhD thesis like nothing's wrong.

Oh, did I mention her thesis has *consumed* our lives? Sticky notes everywhere. Journals? Scattered. *I* could probably defend her thesis by now. I mean, I'm basically an unofficial PhD at this point. So yeah, life is pretty intense at our place.

Now, back to the missed period situation. I gently kiss her on the forehead, because, you know, I'm a good boyfriend. She smiles. *That smile*. The one that makes me forget the world is burning down around us.

Me: "Are you sure it's just stress?"
Prakriti (totally chill): "Gaurav, it's fine. I'm stressed. PhD life, remember?"

Me (trying to act calm, but sweating bullets): "Oh yeah, yeah, of course. I'm not worried. Pfft. Why would I be?"

Pause here, dear reader.

Let's assess: Gaurav is clearly *not* fine. He's trying to act all cool, but we know better. Keep your eyes on him.

But seriously, you know that feeling when everything is going fine, but the universe just loves messing with you? It's like you're waiting for the hammer to drop, but you have no idea when or where it's coming from.

Cue: *The Google Photos Disaster*

Just as I start calming down, thinking, *Hey, maybe I'm overreacting*, Google, our dear overlord, decides to throw gasoline onto the fire.

Ding!

A notification pops up on Prakriti's laptop. *Google Photos Memory*. And guess what memory it's showing? Oh, just a nice little throwback to when I was dating *my ex*. Yep, the snake.

Prakriti (grinning like she's about to drop a bomb): "You guys look cute together."

Me (panicking internally): *Abort. Abort. Abort.*

Now, for the record, this is not a drill. There is no "cute" way to respond to your current girlfriend complimenting photos of you with your ex. Every answer is a potential landmine. So I freeze, like a deer in the headlights.

Prakriti: "Relax, I'm just pulling your leg. I know you had a life before me."

Me (internally sweating bullets): "Right. Haha. Just memories. Totally harmless."

But inside, I'm screaming: *WHY DIDN'T YOU DELETE THOSE PHOTOS, GAURAV?*

And just when I think I'm in the clear, just when I think *maybe* I've dodged a bullet... the Apple ecosystem decides to betray me. (Oh, Apple, you and your sync-everything-everywhere feature. Thanks for that, really.)

Enter: The EX TEXTS

Right on cue, my iPhone lights up, and of course, the message displays on Prakriti's laptop, because why not make this worse? It's from the **ex**. Let's call her "Snake," shall we?

Snake: "Hey, got a Google Photos memory of us!"
Me: *Oh no. Please. Not now. Why now?*

I quickly text back something simple: "I'm sorry, I can't." Trying to end it there. But then, she strikes again.

Snake: "We should meet up sometime! Would be fun to catch up."

This is when the alarms start blaring in my head. I'm frantically tapping out a neutral response, trying to say "no" without setting off any drama bombs. But little did I know... Prakriti is reading **everything**.

Note from the Writer:
It's at this point, dear reader, that we realize Gaurav is in deep trouble. He's swimming in a sea of poor decisions, and the sharks are circling.

Prakriti slams the laptop shut and fixes me with *the look*. You know the one. The one that says, *I'm this close to throwing you and your iPhone out the window.*

Prakriti: "So, you're still talking to your ex?"

Freeze Frame
Gaurav's Mind:

· **What just happened?**

- **Is this real life?**
- **How do I escape this?**

Me, being the genius that I am, stammer: "No, no, she just texted out of the blue!"

Prakriti (unimpressed): "So why didn't you block her?"

And boom. There it is. The bomb has dropped. Prakriti is now the queen of the battlefield, and I am a foot soldier without a shield.

Me: "I—I didn't think it was necessary." (Bad move, Gaurav. Bad move.)

Prakriti: "So you're considering meeting her then?"

Cue the sweating, the internal panic, the complete and utter breakdown of rational thought.

Me (desperately): "No! I'm not meeting her. I just— I didn't want to be rude."

At this point, Hardy is chilling in his tank, probably watching this whole thing like, *Yep, this is gonna end well for you, buddy.* I imagine him munching on some popcorn, enjoying the show.

Prakriti: "Rude? You're worried about being rude to **her** and not about what I think?"

Ouch. Direct hit. I'm scrambling, trying to piece together any coherent defense, but it's too late. The damage is done, and I'm sitting there like a deer in the headlights, hoping the universe throws me a lifeline.

Note from the Write: At this point, Gaurav should probably be sleeping on the couch. But stay tuned—maybe, just maybe, he'll find his way out of the maze.

Day 2: THE AFTERMATH OF "EX-GATE"

After the **EX TEXT** disaster (let's just call it "Ex-Gate" for simplicity), I woke up the next morning to a terrifying realization: I had survived the night, but my relationship? Well, that was another question entirely.

You know that moment when you wake up and for a split second everything feels fine, then BOOM—the memories of last night come crashing down on you like a piano falling out of a 10-story window? Yeah, that was me. Lying in bed, staring at the ceiling, wondering if I could Houdini my way out of this mess.

But first—coffee. Because every decent tragedy needs caffeine.

As I shuffled into the kitchen, I saw Prakriti at the table. She was sipping her own coffee, scrolling through something on her laptop, but there was this *aura* around her, you know? The kind that says, "We're not done here, buddy."

Prakriti (not looking up): "Morning."

Me (nervous): "Morning... how are you feeling?"

Bad move. Too vague. Way too vague.

Prakriti (glancing up, raising an eyebrow): "How do you think I feel?"

Me: *Oh boy, here we go.*

Before I could respond with some lame attempt at deflection, Prakriti set her coffee down and leaned back in her chair. She was calm, too calm. Which is, of course, terrifying.

Prakriti: "I thought about last night. About the texts. About your 'nice' responses."

And this is where I swear my soul temporarily left my body. I could hear the *Jaws* theme playing in the background. Dum-dum... dum-dum...

Me (panicking): "Look, I get it. I should've blocked her. I didn't mean for it to seem like I wanted to talk to her. I just didn't want to be rude—"

Prakriti (interrupting, cool as ice): "Rude? To her? Or are you just too scared to close old doors because it makes you feel better?"

Oof. Direct hit. Ladies and gentlemen, we have entered the **Thunderdome**.

Note from the Writer: At this point, if Gaurav had any survival instincts, he'd throw in the towel and just admit to everything. But, you know him. He's about as sharp as a butter knife in situations like this.

But instead of retreating, I doubled down. Because clearly, I'm a glutton for punishment.

Me: "No! I just didn't want to cause drama. I'm not interested in her, Prakriti. You know that. She's ancient history."

Ancient history, Gaurav? Really? That's the best you could come up with?

Prakriti stared at me, her eyes narrowing, and I could feel the weight of the silence pressing down on my soul. Hardy, meanwhile, was sitting in his tank like a silent witness to my downfall. I swear he was judging me. If turtles could talk, he'd be saying, "Nice going, moron."

THE SILENT WAR BEGINS

Prakriti: "I'm not mad because she texted you. I'm mad because you didn't think of how it would make me feel. I'm your girlfriend, Gaurav. I'm the one who should come first. Not her feelings. Not your need to be 'polite.' Me."

There it was—the truth, plain and simple. And what was I going to say to that? Not much, really. She was right.

I slumped down into the chair across from her, defeated. "You're right," I muttered, feeling like a kid caught with his hand in the cookie jar. "I'm sorry. I should've just blocked her and moved on."

For a moment, I thought maybe—just maybe—things were about to calm down. Maybe we could have a mature, adult conversation about boundaries, trust, and all that grown-up relationship stuff.

Chapter: The Great Misadventure of Gaurav's Tawang Escape

(A story of panic, a surprise ride, and a near-death experience all tied together with a thread of humor and love.)

Alright, dear reader, buckle up, because what you're about to experience is not just a story. No, it's a labyrinth of poor decisions, a sprinkle of bad luck, and a dollop of unplanned chaos.

Let's kick things off with *The Ex*. Yes, because no story would be complete without that lurking figure from the past, casting shadows over the present like a nosy neighbor peering over your fence. So, there I was, trying to handle the situation with my typical level of grace (read: none). After the unfortunate ex-text incident, things were already tense at home. The ex had dropped a casual "Oh, I hope I didn't cause chaos in your relationship" bomb via text, and I blocked her. **Finally.**

But Prakriti wasn't having it. **And rightly so.** She gave me the look, the one that turns your stomach upside down and makes you feel like the world is about to implode. She had every reason to be mad. And what did I do, you ask? Well, instead of facing the music, I pulled the classic Gaurav move—I ran. Literally.

And here's where the universe played its hand in this cosmic joke. I decided to take an impromptu trip to *Tawang*. No plan. No preparation. No oil change on the bike, no weather forecast check, and certainly no common sense. I just packed some random clothes, left a note, and off I went. You know those stories where the hero rides off into the sunset? This was not one of those stories. Spoiler alert: I almost died. Twice.

Day One: Avoidance is Bliss (or So I Thought)

So, there I was, heading toward Tawang, ignoring the fact that I had zero signal and a string of missed calls from Prakriti. In my mind, I thought I was taking the high road—literally—by going off the grid to have some alone time and "think." By the time I reached *Dirang*, everything seemed smooth. No drama, no chaos... yet.

Cue the next day: *The Adventure Begins*.

The ride to *Sela Pass* was straight out of a horror movie. My bike, which I now realize was probably less reliable than Hardy when he's trying to avoid eating his greens, struggled to climb. The fog was so thick I might as well have been driving through a cloud of milk. Visibility? Zero. I was pretty sure Hardy could've crawled faster than I was moving up that pass. **I couldn't see a thing.** Not the road, not the cliffs, and definitely not my sanity slipping away. It felt like one wrong move and I'd be rolling down the mountain, a tragic headline waiting to happen.

But guess what? I made it to Tawang. Sopping wet, freezing cold, but alive. And I couldn't find a place to stay. **Perfect.** Who needs pre-booking, right? I wandered around town like a lost puppy until I finally snagged a room with a heater. Because let's be real, hypothermia was on my to-do list at that point.

The Realization

Sitting in that hotel room, I started to realize how stupid this whole thing was. Running away never solves anything, right? So, there I was, sitting in a monastery the next day, contemplating life, when I finally texted Prakriti:
"I'm returning home from Tawang, sorry for everything."

To my surprise, I saw a bunch of messages waiting for me, each more concerned than the last. I thought I was being brave. Turns out, I was just being dumb.

Prakriti's message popped up:
"I'm not mad at you, Gaurav. I'm sorry too. Just come home safe, I love you."

Cue the tears—because I'm not crying, *you're* crying. Suddenly, all I wanted was to be back home, holding Prakriti. No more dramatic getaways. No more running. Just her.

The Ride Back: The Universe Had Other Plans

You know that feeling when you're so close to fixing everything, and then BAM—Mother Nature decides to slap you across the face? That was me on the ride back. The weather decided to go full apocalyptic. Heavy rain? Check. Fog so thick you could cut it with a knife? Check. But I kept going, hoping to get back to *Dirang* before things got worse. Spoiler: things got worse.

The fog on the road was a scene straight out of Silent Hill. I was honking like a madman and riding slower than a snail in a coma. With each turn, I could feel the boulders looming, ready to roll down and flatten me. At this point, I started praying to every deity I could think of. All I could focus on was Prakriti's face and how much I missed her. **Oh, and not dying.** That was a big one too.

But as if the universe wasn't done laughing at me, I hit a **landslide**. Yep, the road was blocked, and I had no choice but to turn around and take another route. Cue the wet socks, shivering, and mental breakdown as I attempted to retrace my steps through the fog, falling rocks, and, oh yes, more rain.

Finally, after what felt like an eternity, I made it to a new hotel and collapsed. The next day, the weather cleared, and I headed straight home. No detours. No distractions. Just a man on a mission to apologize to the love of his life.

The Reunion

When I finally reached home, I walked in, drenched and tired, and there she was—Prakriti. She didn't yell, didn't give me the cold shoulder. Instead, she hugged me, tears streaming down her face.

"*I'm sorry,*" I whispered, holding her close. "*I love you. I was an idiot.*"

She kissed me and, through her tears, replied, "*I love you too. Don't ever do that again.*"

And just like that, all the drama, all the chaos melted away. We sat down, holding each other, and for the first time in what felt like forever, everything was right in the world.

Note from the Writer:

Dear reader, sometimes love stories need a little extra spice. A dash of chaos, a pinch of poor decisions, and a heaping spoonful of near-death experiences. Because let's face it—no one ever said love was perfect. But with the right person, even the most insane journeys (and the stupidest choices) can lead you back home.

18

Crackers, Balloons, and Unspoken Love

It's been a while since anything particularly exciting happened, but you know what? Prakriti will always be the special one in my life. I could talk about her endlessly—how she's as beautiful as the day I first laid eyes on her, how her smile still makes my heart skip a beat, and those captivating eyes? Let's just say they could stop traffic.

But today? Today is my birthday. And boy, did Prakriti have a surprise in store for me.

The Birthday Surprise

As I stepped out of the apartment, I knocked on the door, and everything was dark inside. Seriously, not a single light was on. Did I just step into a horror movie? Maybe it was a plot twist? Just as I was contemplating whether to call for backup or prepare for an unexpected jump scare, the door swung open.

A soft kiss greeted me, followed by, "Happy birthday, love!"

She looked stunning in her skirt, like an angel who dropped by just to wish me a good one. I mean, if this isn't a

Hallmark moment, I don't know what is.

"Go ahead, blow this out!" she said, handing me a cracker torch with a grin that could melt glaciers. I lit it, and the spark ignited a cascade of colorful lights in the dark room.

"Wow, it's like I'm on the set of a romantic comedy! Where's my soundtrack?"

In response, she reached for the speaker and played some soft background music that seemed perfectly timed, like it was rehearsed for this very moment.

The room was a spectacle of red heart balloons floating above us, and some of them even burst from the cracker fire like they were in on the joke. I glanced at Hardy's tank, and what do I see? Hardy splashing around, clearly excited to join in the festivities. He was practically yelling, "Happy birthday, human!" in his own turtle way.

"Look at Hardy! He's throwing a party in his tank. Should we get him a tiny party hat?"

Laughter erupted. "Only if you promise not to make him wear it. He has enough on his plate—like being the cutest turtle ever!"

I moved into the dining room, where the real surprise awaited. A bottle of red wine, a beautifully decorated cake, and a letter tied with a ribbon sat on the table, flanked by an array of our photos dangling from the ceiling like memories frozen in time.

"You went all out! This is amazing!"

I hugged her tightly, feeling the warmth radiating from her.

"It's nothing compared to what you do for me."

"Please! It's way better than what I could ever come up with."

I reflected on all the surprises I'd given her. They were always nice but, let's be real, totally predictable. But she had a talent for thinking outside the box. It made me feel incredibly special, like I had won the romantic lottery.

"Honestly, I was so terrified to tell you how I felt back then."

"Why? You could've just texted me. You know how good I am at interpreting cryptic messages."

"Yeah, but I was worried you'd see my name pop up and think, 'Oh boy, here we go again.'"

"Well, thankfully you didn't! Because now I get to shower you with birthday love instead."

She planted a soft kiss on my cheek, and I could feel the warmth spread through me, grounding me in the moment.

"You know what? I'm still terrified of my feelings, but you make it all worth it."

"Good! Because I plan to keep doing this for a long time."

I picked up the letter and began to unwrap it.

"What's this? A love letter? Or a 'how to manage your turtle' guide?"

Rolling her eyes, she playfully swatted at me.

"Open it and find out, Mr. Curious."

As I unfolded the letter, I felt my heart race. It was filled with all the reasons she loved me, with personal anecdotes that made me laugh and brought a tear to my eye.

"Okay, now you've officially made me the happiest birthday boy in the universe!"

"That was the plan, genius!"

We ended up sharing slices of cake, our laughter blending with the soft music in the background. I looked at her, and I knew that no matter what else happened in life, this moment was golden—a perfect blend of humor, love, and the occasional splash of turtle chaos.

Note from the Writer:*Dear reader, sometimes love is like a beautifully wrapped gift: full of surprises, laughter, and a dash* *of spontaneity. Here's to our couple, who learned that no matter how many times they stumble through the maze of life, love always finds a way to lead them back home—especially when there's cake involved.*

Epilogue

So, it's been five years now. Yup, five! I know, right? Time flies when you're trying not to screw things up with the love of your life. And in case you were wondering—yes, Prakriti and I are still together, still figuring out how to navigate this whole "adulting" thing without too many bruises.

You remember that girl from the café, right? The one who loved mystery novels, looked cute in glasses, and had a habit of making me question whether I'd ever say something remotely intelligent? Yeah, her. We've somehow survived through all the ups and downs, weird conversations, and Hardy-related shenanigans (side note: our turtle is practically a celebrity in our friend group now—go figure). And before you ask—yes, he still has the occasional escape plan, but we've beefed up security around his tank.

But let me tell you, folks, love is not the fairy tale we all imagine. It's more like an epic comedy-drama where you spill coffee on yourself during a serious moment, or, in my case, accidentally like a two-year-old Instagram post at 2 AM. Trust me, I'm still paying for that one.

Yet, somehow, we made it here. And oh boy, today's the day! The day I pop the big question. I know, I know—I already confessed my love for her on a riverside (as you read about in *Brewing Confessions*—good title, right?). But this one's different. This is **THE** question. "Will you marry me?" You'd think after five years, it'd be easier, but no. My heart is currently doing a drum solo that would make any rock band jealous.

But before we get to that, let me fill you in on how much has changed. First of all, *Dr.* Prakriti is officially in the house! Yep, she defended her thesis today and I swear she looked more like she won an Oscar. She turned to me with those glistening eyes and said, "I couldn't have done it without you, Gaurav." Honestly, I just stood there awkwardly, trying not to cry like I was watching the season finale of some overly emotional Netflix show.

Anyway, I've got the ring, the nerves, and a *half-baked* plan that only involves me dropping to one knee in front of a crowd. No big deal, right? Wrong. It's terrifying. Seriously, why didn't anyone warn me that proposing is ten times harder than confessing your love?

As she's basking in her new doctoral glow, surrounded by all the other brainiacs, I grab her attention. "Prakriti, can I talk to you for a sec?" She smiles—totally unaware that I'm about to throw a plot twist her way.

The sky is putting on its best show—sunset, golden hues, the works. You know the deal, the same setup from *Chapter One.* Yes, I'm being self-referential because why not? This story has been my own personal rom-com, and you, dear reader, have been along for the ride.

"Prakriti," I start, pulling out the ring and kneeling like I've seen in every movie ever. She gasps—yes, actual gasp—and the scholars around us are starting to realize what's happening. Cue the stares. I can hear Hardy's imaginary commentary from back home: *"You better not mess this up, Gaurav."*

"Will you marry me?" I ask, looking up at her, trying to keep my voice steady. Her eyes well up with tears—happy ones, I hope—and she says it, the words I've been waiting for:

"Yes, you idiot, of course I will!"

We're surrounded by cheers from a bunch of nerds in academic regalia, which is the *most* unexpected, and oddly perfect, audience I could've hoped for. She laughs, wipes away a tear, and then, in classic Prakriti fashion, adds, "You know, you could've proposed after I grabbed dinner. Now I'm going to be crying into my pasta."

And just like that, we're laughing again. Because that's what we do—find the humor even in the most intense, heartfelt moments. I slip the ring onto her finger, and for a moment, time really does stop. Or at least it feels like it.

Now, if you're expecting me to say, "And they lived happily ever after," I hate to break it to you, but we all know the real adventure is just beginning. There are *families* to deal with—yes, our families. Let's just say they're not exactly compatible. It's like trying to pair a MacBook with an Android phone—it's possible, but it's going to take a lot of explaining. Spoilers: *Part Two* of this saga will involve dramatic family meetings, awkward dinners, and me trying to win over Prakriti's mom, who, let's just say, isn't my biggest fan... yet.

But hey, if we can survive Hardy's antics, Instagram mishaps, and that time I almost killed us on the bike, I think we can handle whatever comes next.

So buckle up, folks. The ride isn't over. In fact, I'd argue we're just getting started.

Until next time—happy reading, and wish me luck with the in-laws!

Note From The Writer:

Well, here we are, folks—the end of **Part On**e. Can you believe Gaurav finally got his act together and proposed? Took him long enough, right? But don't get too comfortable thinking everything's all wrapped up with a neat little bow. If you've been paying attention, you'll know that this isn't your average "happily ever after." I mean, have you met Gaurav? The man can barely get through a dinner date without overanalyzing his every move, so you can bet his journey is far from over.

I know what you're thinking: **"What's next?"** Well, I won't spoil too much, but let's just say that while love might be simple, **families**are not. Imagine two sets of in-laws with personalities as different as Gaurav's wardrobe (black, black, and more black) and Hardy's diet (lettuce, lettuce, and the occasional sneaky goldfish). Drama, misunderstandings, and humor are all on the horizon—and don't worry, Hardy's going to play a major role in the next act too.

And just between us, if you thought Gaurav was nervous about proposing, wait until you see him trying to survive family gatherings. Spoiler alert: it's going to be awkward.

So, if you're ready for more unexpected twists, awkward silences, and a **ton**of laughs, stick around. **Part Two** is just around the corner, and trust me, the real fun is only beginning.

Stay tuned, folks—this story isn't over yet.

Prakriti,

I know writing a letter is a bit awkward, but I couldn't leave without telling you how much I'm going to miss you. Honestly, I've been staring at this page for way too long, trying to find the right words, but nothing feels quite enough. So, here I am, doing what I do best—rambling and hoping you don't find it too cringeworthy.

Do you remember the first day we met? The café, the book you were reading, that moment when I was completely lost for words? It feels like it was just yesterday, but somehow it also feels like a lifetime ago. Those coffee shop adventures, the long rides, and all those simple, perfect moments—I'm going to miss all of it. Mostly, I'm going to miss you. A lot.

You're easily one of the best people I've ever met. Scratch that—you *are* the best person I've ever met. And spending time with you has been one of the best parts of my life. Everything happened so fast, and now I don't even have the chance to give you a proper goodbye. But knowing me, I'd probably make it awkward anyway, so maybe it's for the best.

Still, it doesn't make leaving any easier. I keep thinking about your smile—that smile that could light up even the dullest day—and how I'm really going to miss seeing it. I wish I could stay, but life, in all its weirdness, sometimes pulls us in different directions. Reality has a way of being annoying like that, right?

But here's the thing—I don't want this to be goodbye. I'll come back to visit you as soon as I can, and until then, I hope you won't forget about me. Don't be a stranger, okay? I mean, you wouldn't want to leave Hardy without his biggest fan, would you?

So yeah, I'll really miss you, Prakriti. And if you ever need me, whether it's to talk, to vent, or to explore another café—I'll be just a call away.

Take care of yourself, and don't let life get too serious. We've still got plenty of sunsets to chase, right?

Yours awkwardly but sincerely,

Gaurav

First Letter From Chapter 8

You have no idea how much I've missed you—no, actually, you probably do, but let me tell you, it's been more than I could ever put into words. Yesterday, when I was riding my bike just to surprise you, the entire journey was filled with one thought: *When will I finally see you?* I was practically counting down the seconds until I could look into your eyes again.

I know, I know—letters are old-fashioned, but they're also where I'm not a complete disaster. It's easier to talk to you like this, without tripping over my words or, you know, turning into an awkward mess. All I can say is, I miss you, *a lot*. Even Hardy misses you—though I think he's mostly concerned about who's going to spoil him with attention if you're not around.

Those long late-night conversations we've had? They're my favorite. I miss our random texts and those moments where it feels like time doesn't even exist. And even though I'm in this crowded city, it doesn't matter, because without you—the person who makes everything brighter—it just feels empty. You're the one who makes it feel like home, even in a city full of strangers.

Missing you,

Gaurav

Second Letter From Chapter 8

Prakriti,

I handpicked every single gift for you with so much love, and I hope they remind you of how much you mean to me. You know, it's funny—I think about all the things I want to say to you, and then the second you're near, my brain just shuts down. It's like, suddenly, I can't find the right words. But trust me, everything I don't say? I feel it.

I just want you to always be happy, Prakriti, and I'll be there with you through all the highs and lows, no matter what. Last night, all I could think about was how much I wanted to skip the whole travel part and just be with you already. Teleportation would really come in handy right about now, don't you think?

Until then, I'll keep counting down the days until we can be together again.

With all my love,

Gaurav

Third Letter From Chapter 8

Prakriti,

I've been thinking about all of our "unofficial dates" lately, and I have to say—I love every single one of them. The way you smile? It honestly makes my day. I don't think you realize how much your presence lights up everything around me. I can't wait for the next one, and the next, and well... *all* of them. If I had my way, we'd be café-hopping all over town, laughing, talking, and making more memories.

Even when you're not near, I catch myself replaying our moments together in my head. I smile to myself like a fool, but hey, that's what you do to me. Your smile—gosh, it's beautiful. It's the kind of smile that makes everything feel right, no matter how crazy life gets.

I really don't want to go back to Guwahati. If I could, I'd find any excuse to stay—wander from café to café with you, just enjoying every moment. But well... you know, *work*. If only teleportation was real, right?

Missing you already,

Gaurav

Letter From Chapter 10

Prakriti,

I know you're going to absolutely *nail* your PhD entrance. I've got so much confidence in you—it's almost like I've already seen you wearing that Dr. Prakriti title, and trust me, it suits you perfectly. You've been preparing for this, and I believe in you more than words can say. Oh, and Hardy? He wanted me to pass along his best wishes too, though I suspect he's more excited about the idea of getting extra snacks when you succeed.

Listen, don't stress yourself out too much, okay? You've got this in the bag. I have full faith in you, and I know you'll come out on top, just like you always do.

And while we're on the topic of wishing—do you know what I miss the most? All the trips we took. The way we'd hop from café to café, exploring new places, and just being in the moment. I find myself replaying those memories over and over again, and all I want is to relive them with you. So, once you're done acing that exam, how about we plan another one of our spontaneous trips? You bring your smile, and I'll bring the coffee. Deal?

Thinking of you,

Gaurav

Letter From Chapter 11

Prakriti,

A *huge* congratulations to you, Dr. Prakriti! I knew you'd do it—I had absolute faith in you, and now here we are. You've officially made it, and I couldn't be prouder. Honestly, I might just be the happiest person on the planet right now. You've worked so hard for this moment, and seeing you enrolled in the PhD program feels like the culmination of everything you've been striving for.

Of course, I'm going to start calling you *Dr. Prakriti* from now on, whether you like it or not. It just sounds so perfect—like it was meant to be. I can't wait for us to start celebrating properly. I'm thinking we kick it off with some serious café hopping, you know, the kind of caffeine overload that might make us question our life choices later. But hey, what better way to celebrate than with coffee and conversation, right?

But, Prakriti, I have to say—the days without you have been rough. There were so many moments where all I wanted was to be near you, to talk to you, to see that beautiful smile of yours that always makes everything better. Now, no more missing you—because anytime I feel that way, I'll just swing by the university to visit Dr. Prakriti in action. It's like I've got an excuse now to see you even more often!

I'm so incredibly happy for you, and I can't wait to see what's next. You've come so far, and I know this is only the beginning of even more amazing things to come. Congratulations again, Prakriti. You deserve every bit of this success.

Missing you, but not for long,

Gaurav

Letter From Chapter 12

Dear Prakriti,

There have been so many sleepless nights thinking about this moment. I've played it over and over in my mind, rehearsed it a hundred different ways, but now that it's here, I'm still in awe. I always dreamed of this day—*this* day—when I would finally have the courage to tell you how I feel. From the very first moment I saw you, I've been mesmerized. Every day since, you've somehow become even more incredible to me.

All those small moments we've shared—the laughter, the late-night talks, your beautiful smile that lights up everything around me—they've filled my life with so much joy. I've watched you dive into your research with that determined look in your eyes, and honestly, it's one of the things I love most about you. Those eyes of yours—they say so much without you having to utter a single word.

Today is such a special day for me. I've been waiting for this moment for so long, and now, it's finally here. If you're reading this letter, it means I've found the courage to do what I've been rehearsing in my head for what feels like forever—I've proposed to you.

Prakriti, I love you. I love you more than I could ever fully express in words. It took me a lot of courage to say it out loud, but it's been the truest thing in my heart from the start. I want to be with you—for now, for always, for the rest of my life. Through all the ups and downs, through everything life throws our way, I want to face it all with you by my side.

I want to grow old with you, Prakriti. I want a life filled with the laughter we've shared, the conversations that last until sunrise, and the quiet moments where just being with you is enough.

So, here it is: I love you, and I want to spend forever with you.

Yours,

Gaurav

Letter From Chapter 14

To the Love of My Life,

Prakriti, I love you more than words could ever express. Can you believe it's already been a year? It feels like just yesterday I saw you for the first time, completely mesmerized. And now, here we are, one year into this beautiful relationship that somehow feels both brand new and timeless.

This past year with you has been the happiest of my life, and every day I'm reminded of how lucky I am to have you by my side. You've been my biggest support through everything, always there when I needed you, always knowing how to make even the worst days better. Honestly, sometimes I think you're an angel who crash-landed into my life by some cosmic accident, and for that, I'm eternally grateful.

Time really does fly when you're with the right person, and I can't wait to make countless more anniversaries with you—each one a new chapter in our love story. Infinite anniversaries, endless moments of joy, and all the happiness I can possibly give you. That's what I want for us.I love you so much, Prakriti, more than I ever thought I could love anyone. You've made my life richer, fuller, and so much brighter. I'm beyond excited for what our future holds, and I promise I'll spend every day trying to give you the happiness you deserve.

Forever yours,

Gaurav

Dear Prakriti,

I'm really sorry if I've hurt you. It was never my intention to say anything that would cause you pain. I've been reflecting on everything, and I realize how important it is to communicate openly, especially with someone as special as you.

I love you—that's the heart of it. But I don't want to fight or let misunderstandings come between us. You mean so much to me, and the last thing I want is for us to be at odds.

I just need a moment to clear my head, to process things, and I hope you can understand that. Please know that my feelings for you remain strong, and I truly want to work through this together.

Let's find a way to talk it out when we're both ready. I care about you deeply, and I'm here for you.

Always,

Gaurav

Letter From Chapter 18

My Dearest Gaurav,

I have to start with a disclaimer: I'm not the best at writing letters, but I promise to pour my heart into this one.You are the most special person in my life, and I can't imagine my world without you. You make me feel safe and cherished every single day. Your laughter lights up my heart, and your kindness wraps around me like a warm hug. Honestly, I feel so incredibly lucky to have you by my side.

I love you more than words can express. Even if my words don't always come out as poetic as I wish, please know that you are my everything. Through all our ups and downs, you have been my rock, and I want you to remember that I will always be there for you, no matter what life throws our way.

I've heard that soulmates are crafted in the heavens and meet on Earth, and Gaurav, I feel so blessed to call you my partner. Our connection is something extraordinary, something I've dreamed about. You are not just my love; you are my confidant, my joy, and my greatest adventure.

Happy birthday once again, my love! Here's to celebrating you today and every day, and to many more memories we'll create together. You deserve all the happiness in the world, and I will do everything I can to give you that.

With all my love,
Prakriti

Bonus Chapter: A Day Of Dreams

The sun peeked through the curtains, and I jumped out of bed, practically buzzing with excitement. Today was our big day—Prakriti and I were going on our first official outing as an engaged couple! I glanced at the ring box on the bedside table, the very same one that had held my heart when I proposed.

(Note to self: Remember to keep the ring box in a safe place, not under the pile of laundry like last time.)

When I finally stepped out of the bathroom, I found Prakriti sitting on the edge of the bed, looking absolutely stunning in her dress.

"Good morning, beautiful," I said, trying to sound smooth.

(Good job, Gaurav. Just don't trip over your own feet!)

"Ready for our adventure, Mr. Future Husband?" she asked, her eyes sparkling with excitement.

"Absolutely! I've got a few surprises up my sleeve," I replied, grinning.

(And by surprises, I mean multiple coffee stops and a picnic, but let's keep that a secret for now!)

We made our way through the lively streets of Tezpur, the aroma of freshly brewed coffee filling the air. Our first stop? The café where it all began.

"Do you remember our first date?" I asked, chuckling.

"How could I forget? You almost spilled coffee all over yourself!" she laughed.

"I still can't believe I was that awkward," I admitted. "But it led us here."

After several cafés and plenty of coffee, I led Prakriti to a lovely park, pulling out a picnic basket like a magician revealing a rabbit.

"Ta-da! Picnic time!" I announced.

Her eyes lit up. "You're full of surprises today!"

"Only the best for my fiancée!" I laid out the blanket and revealed an array of snacks.

(Cue the "awws," readers. This is how you win the heart of your significant other!)

As we shared sandwiches and laughter, I felt so grateful. "Prakriti," I said, "you make me feel loved and safe. I can't imagine my life without you."

"Promise you'll always be by my side?" she asked, her gaze earnest.

"Promise," I said, squeezing her hand.

(And there it is, folks—another heartwarming moment for the story!)

As the sun dipped lower in the sky, I leaned in for a kiss, sealing our perfect day with love.

"Here's to many more adventures together," I whispered.

(Stay tuned, dear readers! There's more to come in our wild love story—just wait for the next chapter of chaos and joy!)

Hidden Letter

My Dearest Prakriti,

As you find this hidden letter nestled in the ring box, I can't help but smile, thinking about the moment I finally confessed my love and asked you to marry me. Let me tell you, it was the biggest, most nerve-wracking confession of my life! It felt ten times harder than any rehearsal I'd ever done. My heart raced as I waited for your answer, and when you said yes, it was like the world lit up around us.

We've come so far together, and our relationship is stronger than ever. Every laugh, every tear, every moment we've shared has woven us closer together, and I cherish every single one of them. Prakriti, as I've always said, I want to grow old with you, and now that dream is becoming a reality.

Sometimes, it still feels surreal to me—like a beautiful dream. I remember that day I first saw you in the café, and how randomly our paths crossed. Who would have thought that a chance meeting could lead to such a profound connection? Now look at us, so intricately entwined in each other's lives, and I couldn't be more grateful.

Prakriti, I love you with all that I am. No words in this world can truly express the depth of my feelings for you. Thank you for being such an incredible part of my life. I promise to always stand by your side, holding your hand through every high and every low, through all the ups and downs that life may throw our way. You are my heart, my soul, and my greatest adventure.

I can't wait to embark on this next chapter together. You mean everything to me, and I am so excited about our future.

With all my love,
Gaurav